ANNE FINE

The Road
of Bones

CORGI BOOKS

THE ROAD OF BONES
A CORGI BOOK 978 0 552 55493 0

First published in Great Britain by Doubleday,
an imprint of Random House Children's Books

Doubleday edition published 2006
Corgi edition published 2007

1 3 5 7 9 10 8 6 4 2

Mixed Sources

Product group from well-managed
forests and other controlled sources

FSC   www.fsc.org Cert no. TT-COC-2139
© 1996 Forest Stewardship Council

Set in 12/18pt Gioconda
By Falcon Oast Graphic Art Ltd

Corgi Books are published by Random House Children's Books,
61–63 Uxbridge Road, London W5 5SA

www.kidsatrandomhouse.co.uk

Addresses for companies within The Random House Group Limited
can be found at: www.randomhouse.co.uk/offices.htm

THE RANDOM HOUSE GROUP Limited Reg. No. 954009

A CIP catalogue record for this book is available from the British Library.

Printed in the UK by
CPI Bookmarque, Croydon, CRO 4TD

As the foreman turned with a finger stretched to point, I felt Karl's hand on me. He was pushing me down behind his freshly laid bricks.

'It's you they're after.'

'Me?'

'Aren't you the one who opened his mouth too wide over his soup?'

'All I said was—'

He cut me off. 'Whatever you said, it was more than enough.' Still holding my head down, he was pulling me over the rough cement floor to the other side of the building, alongside the trees.

'Quick!' he said. 'Get your foot in the bucket.'

'In the bucket?' I peered over the edge. What was he thinking? To lower me over like a load of mortar being sent back down?

I thought he was mad and my face must have shown it.

'Use your wits, Yuri. Either you risk a fall now, or you wait for those men to make even more of a mess of you later, here or in their cells.'

'Cells?'

'Yuri, wake up! You've seen the colour of their uniforms. You know who's coming for you.'

And if I was pale before, now I was grey with fright . . .

For Sophie K.

Note to the reader

I have taken great liberties with history, geography, language and culture.

Nonetheless, inside this story lies a part of the truth.

CHAPTER ONE

My grandmother said it each time. I see her standing beside the cracked iron stove my father half-killed himself in dragging home. In would come the news. 'Chechov is gone.' 'Kerentz has fallen from favour.' 'It seems that Dolov has most conveniently had a "heart attack".' She'd snort with contempt and mutter bitterly into the pots she stirred.

'Only a fool cheers when the new prince rises.'

For years I mistook her meaning. I'd listened to her tales of fair princesses and malignant dwarves, and knew all the old stories about good-hearted giants and ice-crystal palaces hidden in mountainsides. So though I heard it often, her tart remark echoed only in the magically lit cave of my imagination. Gradually the image rose of some young prince rising, freshly crowned, from his throne, and I thought my grandmother was saying no more than that the new ruler's subjects were supposed to know their part of the ceremony was to stay on their knees.

And weren't we all good at that! My father

grumbled to my mother constantly. 'Could we be forced to scrape lower? See? We are beaten to the ground.'

She'd hush him. 'Grigor, I beg you! Not so the boy can hear! And never outside.' For even then there were whispers that people vanished on the way to work, and no one saw and no one heard.

And no one ever came back.

'That,' said my father, 'is because you'd grow a beard down to your feet even in getting there.' ('There' being the far north-east, above the great dividing range and over the frozen bays of Kolskaya and Vlostok, where even the fishing stops for half the year as the waters ice over.) Grandmother would shrug. To her, one prison camp sounded much like another. And to a woman who had never left our province, all places seemed as far away and no further than where the sun sets over the Chelya hills. She'd scrape the skeins of grey mould off the last turnips with a blackened fingernail, and tell for the thousandth time the story that always left her wheezing with amusement, and me in shudders of distress.

'No need to tell the Kulik twins how far to those camps. Poor souls. Alike as two nuts on a twig, but oh, so different inside. Victor now, he was like Yuri here.' She'd tip her thumb at me. 'All ears. All eyes. And always "Why this?", "Why that?" Oh yes, young Victor's brains whirred round all day. But it was Stephan who was the apple of his mother's eye. A soft lad. His only thought was to get down to the river to fish.'

I'd sit with my head well down over my school-book, willing my grandmother to scald herself or cut her finger – anything, even spill the thin soup, rather than go on with the story.

'Then the Czar's men came to arrest young Victor. So there he stood, this captain, reading to Victor's mother from the charge sheet, and she not understanding a word, of course, not being bright or schooled. And he looked up to see her staring at him, all slack-mouthed and drooling from utter fright. "Sedition," he said again, and then took pity on her. "Bare-arsed rebellion," he explained. "Undermining the Czar's authority."'

I hated the story so much, I wanted its telling over. 'So off the soldiers went—'

'So off the soldiers went, to find young Victor. But no one was helpful. Some of the villagers did go as far as murmuring that Victor's twin brother might be down at the river, fishing as usual. But where the lad the soldiers had come to arrest might be, no one would even venture an opinion, for fear they might be right.'

I'd worked out years ago that everyone in the story had to be dead by now. But still my stomach churned.

'And in the end, of course, the captain lost patience. Three hours out of a morning, to find a boy who couldn't grow a beard. "Go fetch the other one," he told his men. And they rode down to the river and took poor Stephan – and his fine fish, they say – and carried him off. Three days later, young Victor came home. His foolish mother must have spat toads at him. "This is your fault! All your fine speeches in the market place! All your petitions and meetings!" Lord knows what curses she must have heaped on his head. All I can tell you is that, within a day, the boy had left the village – gone off to find his brother and exchange himself.'

Again, she'd snort.

'And neither ever came home. More fool their mother!'

For Grandmother, this was the end of a very fine story. She'd cackle away, thinking Victor and his mother prize dolts. (And, as she said so often whenever I cracked a plate or let the fire go out, 'No need to sow fools. Like weeds, they come up of their own accord.') She didn't think, as I did, that maybe Victor had come home, not to a heap of curses, but only to his mother's tears. It never occurred to her that a young man who cared enough about justice and fairness to risk his liberty speaking his mind in the market place and handing out pamphlets might follow his brother willingly over the frozen wastes to try to save him from seven long years of drudgery he hadn't earned for himself.

So I was used to tales of men and women who slid away from towns and villages and hid from the Czar's men for years and years. Some of her stories worried me. But till I went to school, Grandmother's memories of life in her village were much the same to me as tales of pirates and highwaymen and bandits. After all, the Czar was long gone – his throat slit and his family scattered even before the Five Great Leaders signed the Republic into life. ('A fine day!' grinned my father. 'We fooled the class simpleton into believing that all the firecrackers and the flags were there to celebrate his thirteenth birthday.')

In any case, ill luck could fall on anyone. Even in my class at school, there was poor Vladimir with his useless, crippled legs, sweet-natured Ludmilla with her endlessly suppurating face, and Fyodor Kalinsky, whose family all died of cholera within a week, leaving him so shocked and dumb he earned a beating daily.

'A few simple words!' our teacher would howl at him, his nostrils flaring red with rage and frustration. 'Can you not march in time and get a few simple words in the right order?'

We'd raise the banners and start to practise the anniversary procession again.

'On this great day, we hail Our Beloved Leaders, and step out willingly on the Long March to a Better Future for All.'

Fyodor would only tremble. At times, his tears ran. Sometimes his face became so blank you'd think he'd gone deaf as well as silent. In the end, one of the other teachers would pull him aside and leave him standing while we marched briskly up and down on the packed snow, and Fyodor froze faster than his banner.

Those banners! Half our lesson time was taken up with cutting them out and printing the words. Before I was even seven, I swear I could spell "The Glorious Revolution". ('"The Glorious *Lie*", more like,' my grandmother muttered with a scowl the day they told us that part of our family's contribution to the Next Steps for Progress was to share the floor of our block with three other families.)

So there was always schoolwork to do in the evenings to make up for the hours spent on our flags and parades. And nowhere to do it away from Grandmother and her stories. I suppose that, to someone standing stirring away the rest of her life, old times are all that's left. So as I sat over our brand-new history book, learning about all the countries around us that had welcomed our soldiers with songs of liberation and bright spring flowers, her witterings dripped into my brain. I didn't listen, but every few minutes my ears would unstop enough to hear yet another snippet from Grandmother's village childhood.

'And by the time he was released, of course, his mother was dead.'

'After seven years, she despaired and married someone else, only for him to arrive the next morning, footsore and bleeding.'

'And he never came back.'

'Stop with the tales!' I remember my mother once begging her. 'Just for one night, can we sit and eat without the troubles of the world heaped on our plates as well?' She looked at my father as if to say, 'Support me here, Grigor. This is *your* mother, not mine.'

But he was flicking through *The Wonderful Story of Our Motherland*, his eyebrows raised. 'Is this what they're telling you now? Our soldiers welcomed with songs and flowers?' Dropping his voice to a whisper, he turned to my mother. 'Best not tell Grandmother! Or she might wonder what sort of flower it was that blew out her husband's brains.'

'Hush, Grigor! Not in front of Yuri!'

But I'd been deaf so often from colds and agues when I was smaller that they were easily fooled by a blank face. And as soon as they thought I was asleep under the rugs, their whisperings would start again – and these were not old tales like Grandmother's, but things that had happened only that day to some journalist who had written of one of the Five Great Leaders with too sharp a pen, or to the editor of some journal called *New Directions* or *A Better Path*.

One night the news came from so close to home, my mother couldn't wait for a prudent time to tell it. Seeing my hands were over my ears as usual while I was reading, she risked saying softly to my father, 'Novgorod's gone.'

'Novgorod?'

'Yesterday evening, they came.' She shook the snow crystals from her headscarf towards the fire, making it hiss and spit. 'Through a mercy his boys had gone off early, so there was only him beside the printing press. The guards broke up the type. Natasha says he smashed his own spectacles trying to stop them. And then two of the taller ones lifted poor Novgorod between them, arm in arm, and carried him off. Natasha's mother said his legs were so far off the ground he looked like a child refusing to go to the priest for a blessing.'

My father frowned. Since all the churches had been sacked and locked, even second-hand talk of priests was unwelcome. 'Any word from him since?'

'Nothing. He shouted down the empty street, of course. "Keep up the work! Keep up the work!"' She stared at the one smoking ember in the grate and added bitterly, 'A fine message to leave the neighbours to pass to your sons. Practically a death sentence.'

My father tried to comfort her. 'No, no. Their mother won't let them take the risk. She was against the business of the journal from the start.'

They shook their heads, and spoke of passing the news to friends the very next morning. And as the tale of Novgorod's arrest spread out from those who knew each other well to those who barely nodded in the street, no doubt fewer and fewer dared venture the general opinion: 'What sort of idiot can't tell the difference between the "right to publish" and a steel-capped boot?' But back then everyone who'd been told would at least dare to slow their stride next time they passed the kiosk where *People Before Party* had been heaped in a pile, fruitlessly waiting for customers. I expect that, to some, it barely seemed possible that the earnest, owl-eyed man someone had pointed out to them once in a teashop was even now rattling his way in chains towards some prison camp.

'Oh, he'll be back,' my grandmother would scoff on such occasions. 'The fighting kitten's not so easily drowned.'

And in her day, perhaps, most did come back, even if it was years later, and perhaps with a foot gone from frostbite that ran too deep, or one arm swinging uselessly, from being the worst person in the world to trade a journalist's pen for a prison axe. '*They* recognize *you* first,' she told me once. 'Always. There you are, hurrying down the street with your basket, and you sense something in a stranger going past.'

'What *sort* of something?'

Grandmother had no education ('Nor any brains,' my mother always said, 'if she can cling to all that mumbo-jumbo about God and his saints'). So all she could do was turn from her pots and show me: first, a flicker across the face, then a questioning look; a moment of hesitation.

She picked up her story. 'You peer at the stranger more closely. "Can that be *Leonie*?" you ask yourself. "There's no longer a picking on her!" Or, "How could a bear like Boris come to look such a *splinter*?" You say their name. And when they see that you're not going to walk straight past, their tears well over, and they clasp you so tight you'd think it was you, not them, who'd been away so long up where the nights are white.'

'White nights?'

'In summer. So far north. And black as pitch all winter. Oh, a terrible place to count out seven years with the blows of a pick, then come back to find your family scattered and your life's work gone.'

'Lucky to come back at all,' my mother muttered. She didn't think I heard. But it made no difference in the end because, slopping food from the pot to the dishes, Grandmother emptied enough of the sludge of her spirits on us all to last the whole meal through:

'In this benighted country, you can call no man lucky till he's dead.'

CHAPTER TWO

I don't remember noticing when things began to change. I knew one of the Leaders had been accused of doing his utmost to wreck the Glorious Revolution, and had been sent to an ignominious end, hanging from his heels. (How all my school-mates cheered. How hard we waved our flags. How grateful we were to see the traitor and all his sly henchmen winkled from where they'd been hiding.) I knew our nation's saviours had warned us that there were more enemies of the state still to be rooted out – we must be vigilant, *vigilant* – and that the path of Our Long March now ran through rivers of blood. I knew that we faced enemies on all but one of our borders, and that the army had become as hungry for men as we were for something – anything – more than the meagre ration of herrings and beans and mouldy root vegetables.

So it seemed natural that my parents worked longer and longer hours. The day the china studio was closed ('Uneconomic frivolity!'), my mother found herself on the list of common workers sent to one of the new munitions factories springing up around us. My father's shifts at the sawmill were extended by hours. Even my grandmother suffered. Now, far from spending her days warming her fingers by prodding the stubborn vegetables that stuck to the bottom of her pans, she took to trailing round the town in search of wood to burn or queues to join where there were rumours of food.

Dragging me with her, she did her best to stand up to shopkeepers who quickly learned which customers could slip them a few extra coins for better produce, and which couldn't.

'Your weights are short. And look at these turnips you've given me! They're soft with rot.'

The shopkeeper leaned over the counter to sneer. 'I can see you were raised on milk and gingerbread. Take it or leave it. That's all there is.'

We had no choice. Already he'd snatched her ration paper and rammed it down on his spike. Even if she could persuade him to give it back, no other shopkeeper would dare take it.

Furious, Grandmother spat an insult back. 'Easy enough to be Man of Thunder behind your counter along with all the food. Try joining us here in the queue. You'll soon find out you're nothing but a common cur!'

He thrust his greasy face closer, oozing threat. 'Are you dissatisfied with what your country has to offer you?'

Grandmother stiffened. Perhaps she sensed what I saw – that people who'd been standing in line behind her in the face-biting wind for two full hours were suddenly melting away as if they'd that very instant decided their family had no need of food that day. Coming to her senses, Grandmother grabbed my arm and moved as quickly as her stiff legs could carry her, not towards home, but up one alley and down another, and in and out of courtyards, till she was sure no one was following.

Then, gasping until she breathed more easily, she raised her wrinkled monkey face to look me up and down as if to check I really were no longer the little boy whose hand had to be held the whole way home.

'Go on ahead,' she told me.

'Why?'

'"Why? *Why*?"' Sheer irritation made her slap out at me. 'Must you always be wise as a tree full of owls? Stop asking questions! Do as I say! Go home.'

I didn't argue. The way led past Alyosha's house. He'd been my friend as long as I could remember.

We had a thousand ways of passing time together. In summer we chewed stalks on the canal bank. In winter he let me take turns on his sled with him and his sister. Always, at school, we fought to sit side by side. Ordered so firmly home, I didn't think I'd dare knock on his family's door. But maybe he'd be in the street, out on some errand, and we could spend a bit of time down at the river watching the breaking ice float past in giant lumps.

He wasn't there. I kicked a stone past his door, and back again. But in the end I gave up and hurried home, and it must have been a couple of hours or more before it even struck me that Grandmother must have sent me on ahead for fear the shopkeeper would call for the guards. If they were looking for the pair of malcontents the shopkeeper had described, all they would come across was an idle lad trailing his way home from school and, a street or so over, some ancient biddy trudging back all alone from the market.

Never before had I seen Grandmother so pale from a spat with a shopkeeper. Or scurrying down alleys. But still I didn't realize how much the world around us was changing, or how our lives were shrinking by the day, until the evening I slapped my last ace down on hers and, for the first time ever, got to crow back at her the boast she always made the moment her cards trumped mine:

'For some, the crystal stair! For others, just the road of bones!'

My mother smiled. 'Has Yuri grown up enough to beat you at last? Or are your brains going soft?'

'Neither,' snapped Grandmother. 'It's just that, with the boy being cooped up so much, he's turning into a cardsharp.'

I looked up. Sure enough, the shutters were open to catch the last of the evening breeze. It was still light. Why wasn't I outside, racing along the canal bank with Alyosha, or looking for mischief up back streets?

Because no one roamed now. It wasn't just the splatters of gunfire heard from other streets, or even the occasional dull crump of explosions echoing across the city. It was a creeping sense of fear that had turned all our lives into one long, long wait.

And fed suspicion. I sensed my parents no longer trusted my blank face when they were whispering. I noticed their friends stopped coming to the house, and I was no longer welcome knocking on other people's doors, even Alyosha's. But though I must have asked a host of questions over that long, dreary autumn, my parents' answers were evasive and guarded. And, looking back, I think I must still have taken everything around me for granted, as if the four of us had always spent the gloom of each evening crammed in that tiny room, elbowing for space and trying not to fight for the last shadow of potato.

And some things scarcely changed. The schoolroom was still the schoolroom, for all that the stove was rarely lit now, even on the coldest days. Beatings still fell on us for the same sins: stupidity, fighting, throwing dice in the schoolyard and quarrelling over the lightest banner for the endless parades in honour of the Motherland.

But still, I must have been blind. It was Alyosha who, nudging my elbow one morning, nodded across the room.

'Look.'

Another of the portraits on the wall had vanished overnight. But even when I burst in with a message at break time to find our teacher still carefully razoring that same leader's face out of our textbook, I thought so little of it I didn't mention it at home – not even though that day it was once again my turn to take the precious volume home.

It was my mother who, flicking through silently, caught her thumb on the cut edge.

'What's this?'

Her eyes slid down the page to where one sentence now fell into space and another began in the middle.

Her smile was bitter. 'Ah! So the whispers are right. Now we are down to three . . .'

'Lily!' my father hissed.

I noticed no more than that it used to be *her* who scolded *him* for speaking too openly. Now he was just as keen on hushing her. But most of the time when I was in the room, they rarely spoke, except to rail about the cold when the vast communal boiler in the basement broke down for the tenth time in a week. Or to complain of their hunger after the meat ration, pitiful as it was, was halved yet again.

'When will they realize empty sacks can't stand upright?'

'My belly already thinks my throat's been cut. And now this!'

I sat, unquestioning as a dolt, while the grumbling went on around me, poring over *The Wonderful Story of Our Motherland* in the dim light.

What set me thinking was the song we all knew:

Fairest of Lands, your power shines
Over your mountains and across your seas . . .

Grandmother sang it under her breath when she was busy with a broom, or scrubbing the table. She claimed she'd learned it at her father's knee. He was as proud of his country as any man, and it was a party trick of his to set her before the other villagers on holidays and festivals, to lisp this old favourite.

'I sang it faultlessly,' she boasted. 'Even getting the list of nations in the right order. For years after I grew, people would wink and smile. "Remember how your proud father would stand you on a table to sing it? His two great passions together: country and child."'

Mother and Father had learned the song nearly thirty years later – she at her school in town and he in his village. They'd met when she'd come with some of her Pioneer friends to help with the harvest. ('Spy for the Revolution,' my father always teased. 'See where we hid our grain in case the Leaders decided to steal it later.')

They fell in love. ('Canoodled in the granary,' Grandmother muttered sourly.) Finally, Grigor summoned the courage to ask his sweetheart to stay.

'Why?' Lily asked him.

'So we can be together.'

Scornfully she'd looked him up and down. 'But you're only fifteen.'

His face grew red. 'Grown enough for you all summer!'

Lily relented. 'Come to the town,' she said. 'Join us. Everything we've been telling you is true. We're changing the world there – getting rid of corruption and injustice and starting everything afresh so it'll be fair for all.'

My father was startled. He'd heard her praising the Five Great Leaders often enough over the threshing. But he'd not realized she cared about the Revolution so much she'd expect him to abandon everything he knew to join her in the city. He'd never left the village in his life. He'd sat beside her at the end of the day as she talked so eagerly of women's rights, equality between the sexes and her commitment to the Great March to Our Glorious Future. But he had taken it much as he took the burbling of a stream. Talking was what women did. He'd been too busy watching the way the firelight shone on the wisps of hair that strayed out from under her red bandanna. He hadn't actually *listened*.

'You were a *fool*,' my grandmother spat at him once through her tears, the day the Three Leaders signed in the 'Fifty Mile' rule that meant that neither she nor he would ever see the village again. 'When you were deciding whether or not to follow Lily to the city, you asked yourself the wrong question. Not, "Do I *want* to do this?" Only, "Do I *dare*?" '

And yes, of course, with such a challenge set himself, he'd jumped a train within a week. He tracked down Lily from her careless scribblings on the scrap of paper she'd left him. ('Even the street name was wrong.') And when he finally found her, she was already in bed with someone else. 'I slammed the door and sat against it so neither he nor she could go out without stepping over me.'

Lily let Grigor in. 'Just till you find a place of your own. I'm with Constantin now.' But within a week Constantin had given up coming. Each time Lily came back from a meeting, Grigor was still there. One night she let him into her bed again and, next morning, told him what a disgrace it was for a healthy young man to waste a single day when he could be out there helping to build the brave new world.

'I went off singing that morning,' he told me drily. As if to prove it, he began to belt out the old song that had become our nation's anthem since the real one had been declared 'backward and counter-revolutionary' for mentioning the Czar. ('They've had the man's head off,' Grandmother muttered scornfully. 'Why fret about his hair?')

The first few lines are easy enough and my father made no mistakes singing them:

> *'Fairest of Lands, your power shines*
> *Over your mountains and across your seas.*
> *Cradle of Peace, what nations do you bind*
> *In brother love? Dear Mother of my heart,*
> *I count them for thee.'*

Everyone gets that far. But then my father spun confidently into the part that's difficult: the list of all of the countries bound in brother love that make us such a great land – verses full of strange names, where you can be all too easily tricked by the tune into skipping a republic or two.

My father never faltered, but came to a resounding finish at the end of the third verse.

I knew the song as well. We'd sung it twice a week in Pioneers since I was eight years old. First we'd be sent to gather wood for the fire (before the order filtered down that that was treason against the state, and we just shivered). Then we'd form lines, and march up and down behind the ramparts of heaped snow, singing the anthem and slapping ourselves to its beat to try to keep from freezing. I had a good memory and sang it as unthinkingly as a bird. The names of the republics sailed out of my mouth in perfect order. (When commissars came, I'd always been the one chosen to sing the anthem in the long ceremonies of respect, and no one was jealous because they all knew that a single small slip would have earned them a beating.)

But where we all stopped singing made me curious. It sent me back to my books. And to my teachers. That week, I must have asked a hundred questions. (Easy enough, once you've an interest.) This country is so huge that, if you sent word to the furthest parts, for months you'd have no idea whether you'd lost the message or the messenger. Line us all up, and you'd not believe we are one nation. You would see men in beards, and men for whom even the sight of hair on the face of a man is an abomination. At one end we have women dark as nuts, and at the other, women white as lard. We have whole lands of different peoples: merry and taciturn, careless and ardent. In this great country there will be people going to bed while others are rising. There will be people freezing from the cold while others are parched from the heat, and villages that starve while other villages are packing away the grain for seven years.

And few will know the slightest thing about each

other. So it was easy to intersperse the things I wanted to know ('How many?' 'When?') with the things that I didn't ('And do they wear the same sorts of clothes as us?' 'And is their gruel made out of oats, like ours?') and, over the days and weeks, gather a list of numbers – numbers so huge they'd make your hair stand on end.

When I was ready, I lifted my head from my books at last. 'Go on,' I ordered my family. 'Sing the anthem. All together. The anthem.'

'Go bother someone else,' my mother said. 'I have no time for singing.'

'Hush, Lily!' said my father, glancing at the wall we now shared with the Litnikovs. Clearly he feared that, if she were overheard, she might be thought 'unpatriotic', and rumours were coming in that more people than you might have guessed were being arrested under the new Acts of Loyalty signed in that summer.

I made the most of my father's uneasiness.

'The anthem's different!' I said loudly, almost nodding towards the thin wall. 'Let's sing it as we think of Our Leaders.'

They stared. But now they had no choice. Only that week the papers had praised a man to the skies for boring a tiny hole to eavesdrop on the neighbours he suspected of plotting to wreck the Next Great Step Forward.

So we all sang the song we'd learned so thoroughly – Grandmother over sixty years ago, my parents thirty years back, and me only a few years before.

And it was exactly as I had thought. Grandmother sang along cheerfully and stopped where she always had, at the end of the second verse. Mother and Father kept on for one single verse more before they came to a halt.

And only I could keep the song up through the last eight lines.

I lowered my head to my books again. Maybe they thought that, having wreaked my mischief, I'd returned to my lessons. But not a bit of it. I was copying out figures. How many lived in this republic here? How many Kurds were there? How many Tartars? How many Yuseks had we liberated on the western front? How many Germanics had the annexation of Sirelia brought us?

And the numbers! The numbers!

This 'Cradle of Peace' in which I lived had, it seemed, since my grandmother's childhood, added at least two hundred million souls.

Two hundred million souls!

CHAPTER THREE

So am I sly? Because I said nothing to my parents or
grandmother. I just started to think about this
'Fairest of Lands' of ours, and open my eyes a little
wider. I saw the rags on our beds. The mouldy
turnips in our pot. The glances between my parents
whenever a slogan exhorting us all to even greater
efforts went up on one of the factory chimneys we
could see from our window, or news came in of yet
more wreckers unmasked. ('What's to wreck?'
Grandmother asked sourly, using a filthy old foot-
cloth to coax our last handleless pan away from the
fire.)

I looked out of the same old window, but now I
saw things very differently. Where I'd seen busy
people scurrying to work with their heads down
against the wind or sleet, now everyone looked
furtive. I watched the endless parades and, instead of
admiring the banners, I noticed the dutiful faces
beneath them, the glances at clocks and the im-
patient stamping. I'd nudge Alyosha off the same old

steps and wonder, as he pulled me after him, if he was still as carefree as he seemed. Or if, like me, he had no words for what was going on around us, and, like me, had been learning through his skin that he and his family would be safer if there were never any words at all.

One night I was woken by the sound of shouts in the street. My mother's face was turned to the wall. Was she asleep, or pretending? My father's eyes too were closed and Grandmother snored deeply in the chair.

I slid out from under my rugs, and moved to the shutters.

Instantly my father's eyes snapped open. 'Yuri! Step back!'

But I'd already seen a woman pushed roughly into the back of a car, her shoe left in the gutter, and knew the news would trickle back of yet another saboteur found on our street. I wondered how I could have been so stupid for so long. Why had I never before looked at my mother and asked myself how someone who'd once sat in firelight and talked of the Revolution with shining eyes could turn into someone who, when the third Leader in a row was denounced as a traitor, did no more than murmur, 'Fine ravens, pecking out each other's eyes!'

My father too I saw with clearer eyes. This man who'd joked so cheerfully of the revolutionaries creeping back the moment it suited them to steal his family's grain had turned into a man too timid to speak his thoughts aloud.

But then, who did? No one I knew. Even my grandmother no longer dared so much as nod a greeting to the old biddies she used to stand beside in church, mumbling the prayers my mother said simply distracted fools from changing the real world they lived in to something halfway as fine as the imaginary world they hoped to reach. Only behind our shutters was Grandmother brave enough to make her old proud claim – 'They'll not waste fifty grams of lead putting a bullet in this old brain' – and carry on telling the stories I had been hearing all my life.

But I had changed too. Now, as each story tumbled out of her, I took the time to listen.

'. . . And as the Czar's men caught hold of him, he lifted the handles of his barrow and sent his cabbages rolling down the hill, shouting, "Come, good neighbours! A free cabbage for everyone! And two for the louse who snitched on me!" And, before you could turn, the street was filled with men and women chasing down the hill after the cabbages. But even those who got there first and carried baskets with them took no more than one, for fear they would be thought the traitor who betrayed him!'

Like everyone else my age, I had been taught that the Czar was a monster, a tyrant born to suck his people's blood. But truth trickles out through a crack.

Grandmother noticed me staring. 'Yuri?'

My mother too glanced at me. 'Yuri? Why so pale?'

I shook my head. 'Nothing.' But I was thinking, Now, when the soldiers come, everyone vanishes. No one would stay to chase a cabbage down a hill.

And how quickly the threads had tightened. It seemed no time at all since Alyosha and I were jumping over Novgorod's pamphlets heaped by the kiosk on our way to school. Who, now, would even dare lean out of the window to hear the message the owl-eyed printer had shouted out for his sons, or to see how he broke his glasses, or what he looked like as he was carried away?

No one.

The kiosk was long gone. These days, I thought, as soon as anyone hears the tramp of soldiers, they latch the shutters tight and hide in their beds. No one sees anything. No one dares hear a thing.

Next morning I asked Alyosha in an idle voice, 'Remember Novgorod?'

Instantly he peeled away from my side and down the nearest alley. I hurried after. He began to run. I trapped him in a doorway. His face was pale.

'Agreed!' I said. 'Agreed!'

His breathing slowed. His colour rose again, and after a moment of thinking, he bit his lip and nodded. There was no need to say what had been settled between us. I didn't ask Alyosha what horrors in his street – or family – had set his nerves so on edge he'd end a friendship rather than hear a word about a man who'd once gone a step too far. And he didn't volunteer to tell me.

But curiosity is a weed that spreads. One night I said to my father in what I again pretended was idle innocence, 'What if the last two Leaders should fall out?'

'Yuri,' my father warned. Already his eyes were shifting to the door as if on the other side there might be someone with his ear to the wood. 'Show more sense, son. Keep your eyes down and your ears closed, and we will all be safer.'

'But,' I persisted, 'no one imagined of the other three that they would prove to be traitors. So what's to say—?'

I got no further. The breath was knocked out my body. I found myself against the wall. One of my father's fists was close to my face, the other hand clenched round my throat.

'Enough!' he hissed in my ear. 'Not a word more. Your mother and I haven't crawled like grubs all these long years to have you risk our skins now. This room of ours does not exist, you understand? It might as well be invisible. We wish it were. Your grandmother's just some bumbling fool who scours the market for food we can afford. Your mother works like an automaton at the factory. She has no thought except to fill her quota of bullets like a good daughter of the state and get to the end of her week. And me? I have no opinions at all. I am a hollow man. I cut my lengths of wood exactly as I'm ordered. I ask no questions and I have no views.'

He loosened his grip enough to let me take a breath. But he kept on. 'And that, Yuri, is how we have survived this nightmare so far. That's why your mother isn't in a wagon rolling north, and I'm not lying with a bullet in the back of my head. That's how we stay alive. And that's how we intend to carry on.'

'All right!' I pushed him off. 'All right!'

'So no more talk of our remaining Leaders, except to say they are the fine protectors of their people.'

I nodded. He'd at least offered me the dignity of

letting me know that I was right. 'Nightmare', he'd called it. But it was a clear enough warning. And I am grateful because it did make me wary. I waited longer and I listened more.

And what I learned was something curious. That how you listen matters. Listen in one way and all you hear is praise and gratitude for whatever comes. Listen in another, and things appear in quite a different light.

The very next week, at Pioneer training camp, Alyosha threw down his wooden rifle at the end of the practice and rubbed his shoulder.

'I'm so stiff the pains are running up as high as my ears.'

Sergei, the team leader chosen for his devotion to the troop commissar, promptly rebuked him. 'Alyosha, when our turn comes to defend the Motherland, the rifles we carry will weigh a whole lot more than these.'

Behind me, a soft voice said: 'If we have rifles at all.'

Sergei spun round at once. All of us knew whoever had spoken was on dangerous ground. The troop commissar didn't thank us for making jokes about our wooden weapons. That sort of thing was seen, not as high spirits, but as simple mockery – offensive to the state and showing a lack of respect for all those fighting on our borders, whom we would join one day.

'Who said that? On your feet, whoever said it!'

'I said it.'

The lanky boy who rose left only the shortest pause before carrying on with a broad smile. 'Haven't you heard, Sergei, of the glorious way the Thirteenth Volunteers served the Motherland? It seems they were mustered from their towns and villages in a great hurry and found themselves marched, without any boots or weapons, straight to the battle front. They asked their commander, "But where are our guns?" And he pointed over the ridge to the trenches where the enemy lay waiting. "There are your weapons, boys. Now go and fetch them."'

I stared. The lanky boy reminded me of someone, but I couldn't think who till he reached up with both hands to push his cardboard helmet further back on the mop of his hair. He looked like the monk in one of Grandmother's pictures – the print my father lifted off the wall and burned for safety the day we heard that the empty churches were to become prison pens. I'd stared at the print so often as a child I could remember, clear as paint, the look of bliss spread over the holy man's face.

The boy's smile widened and his bright eyes danced.

He'd better take care, I thought. If Sergei realizes this is a tease, he'll find himself in deep trouble. If I had had more courage of my own, I might have pitched in to join him. After all, I could have asked, 'And did the soldiers triumph? What happened when these barefooted men walked, unprotected, over no man's land towards the enemy's tanks?' But though this lanky boy had somehow managed to wriggle out of his first defeatist remark by telling this brave tale, I knew I didn't have his wits.

So I kept quiet. But later, as we jostled for our bowls of thin soup, I pushed to a place by his side. All evening I waited, hoping he'd say another word to offer a clue to his feelings. He might have fooled Sergei. But I could scarcely doubt that this smart, confident boy's hunch mirrored mine – that, when it was our turn to join the fight, we'd be no better equipped than we were now with stupid wooden sticks.

All the last day I watched him. He dug as hard as I did. He cut as many logs. He argued for his full share of the few lumps of gristle that swam in the gruel, just like the rest of us. He gave out no sign at all that he was different. Once or twice he caught my eye, but only in the way of any boy working close to another.

Finally the time came for us to climb on the wagons, to go back to our towns and villages.

'Who's for Radicz?' shouted one of the drivers.

I saw the boy lift his bundle to his shoulder. On an impulse I turned towards him and stepped in his path. 'Tell me your name.'

The moment the words were out of my mouth I regretted them. I thought he would assume I was one of the boys they set in every troop of Pioneers to eavesdrop and tell tales.

But, if he did, he showed no sign of it. He smiled the open smile I'd seen all week. 'Nikolai,' he told me, and turning away, he swung his bundle up onto the wagon, then used a spoke of the wheel to clamber up beside it.

'Yuri,' I told him in exchange.

CHAPTER FOUR

It was the oddest thing. From that day on, this Nikolai was my very picture of the ones I was looking for – the people I knew must be out there somewhere. People who, like my mother, no longer believed – or, like my grandmother and father, never had been green enough to believe – that this long bloody march of ours would lead to a shining future.

I kept my eyes open for their tracks. And now I was paying attention, every once in a while I'd spot the faintest signs of opposition. Along a wall I'd see a scrubbed and scraped look that hadn't been there the day before, and guess the street commissar had had to remove some hastily painted slogan. Once, on a factory chimney, I saw a few frayed threads, and knew that some brave soul had fixed a counter-revolutionary flag so high that whoever was ordered to fetch it down had finished the job in too great a hurry to pull away the last scraps of cloth.

I couldn't stop and stare. Just to have slowed my pace would have invited trouble. ('Why would you notice the torn threads left by a flag if you'd no connection with the saboteurs who hung it there?') But over the next few days I walked past the brick factory half a dozen times, until at last the harsh spring light fell on the chimney in the right way at the right time.

Yellow and black. The colours of resistance?

Yellow and black.

Next came the summer of the Emergency. We hardly dared go out of the door for the rattle of gunfire. Now everything was rationed: candles, fuel, salt, lightbulbs – even soap and string turned into luxuries. On the worst days I found myself chewing a rag to stave off my hunger. Finally the skirmishes stopped, and we no longer heard the sound of tramping boots below our window.

A week or so later, school opened again.

Grandmother took no interest in which of the last two portraits had come down from the wall. 'Why should I care when one hard wedge knocks out another?'

But it turned out our saviour was Father Trofim. And very soon, from knowing little about him, all of us could have written a book about his life and his virtues. We knew that he'd been born into poverty.

His father was crippled and his mother had died giving birth to a sister. We learned that from the age of six he'd been raised in an orphanage. He had, they told us, always been an excellent pupil. 'The cleverest boy any of his teachers had seen.' We knew he'd been pressed into the army at fourteen and covered himself in glory there as well, winning more medals than all the other officers in his company several times over.

And it was here that he'd come to see the days of the Czar were over. He'd led the struggle. His was the vision and the strength, not just to start the Revolution in the first place, but to keep it rolling.

And now he wore his triumphs modestly. His generals were said to worship him. He loved little children as much as they loved him, and we were shown photographs of boys and girls dancing round his throne-like chair and hurling petals. Soon we knew the date of his birth better than we knew our own, and that, if we followed him faithfully with all our hearts and minds, then our beloved nation would very shortly—

A crock of shit! Simply to let it spill from the tongue was to see it for what it was: nonsense and lies. If Father Trofim was such a hero, such a fine and generous man, why had so many vanished? Why was the struggle so bitter, with rumours of families being uprooted from farms they'd lived on for a hundred years, and villages razed to the ground? We were supposed to praise the Great New Towns of Hope that had sprung up all over. But, in them, everyone was working till they dropped. There were so many arrests that even trusted neighbours had taken to telling tales and even spinning lies to try to curry favour with the guards and save some hot-headed son or daughter of their own found with the recently outlawed yellow and black.

Now, when I sang the anthem, I was terrified, knowing the commissars had taken to proving their loyalty to Father Trofim by finding traitors behind every bush. One little slip would single me out. Then, when more names were needed for the next list of 'troublemakers', it would be me and my family who sprang to mind. There was a whisper running round of one small girl whose hair turned white overnight when they chose her to dance for Father Trofim. And even in our school Oleg ran off, simply for being picked to carry a wreath to one of the memorials. (His family paid heavily for that. The last that was heard of them was a scuffle on the stair, a few stifled cries and the slam of a car door.)

But no one ever saw a thing. Whenever the

soldiers came, you'd think the people they took away with them were the last living creatures in town. Wiser that way. By then, we were all so frightened, the simplest truth couldn't be said aloud.

Except by Grandmother.

'Here is a man who has learned, if you beat a dog hard enough, all you will have to do after that is show him the whip end.'

One week, in school, the top two classes were asked to rise. A Diktat was read out. Once, I had barely listened when we were gathered to listen to these bloated pro-nouncements. Now they all interested me. Some were new rules (the Diktats). Nobody was to walk on the river paths. Rail journeys for mere pleasure were now forbidden. Everyone must take their papers to the street commissar to be checked yet again.

Some were called 'Explications'. From these you might learn, for example, that if you had thought that having a ration book in your own name entitled you to food of your own, you were mistaken. Everyone under sixteen was supposed to be fed out of the share for their parents.

Then there were the Exhortations. These, it appeared, were written by Father Trofim himself. One week we'd hear the story of how some child had written a forty-page poem called 'Our Great Captain' in his praise. A week or so after, it might be some tale of inspirational sacrifice: a group of miners who had offered to work one week in every three without pay for the sake of the Next Great Step Forward; a woman who'd found money in the gutter and, rather than use it to feed or clothe her own family, had sent it to Father Trofim. Even, once, the tale of a little girl of only eight who, hearing her parents speak critically of Father Trofim, had slipped from the house and along to the police in order to denounce them. (I had expected quite a different ending to this story. While not exactly believing that little Yelena would have been packed off home with a flea in her ear and a lecture on family loyalty, still I was shocked to hear that Father Trofim had personally pinned on her Pioneer uniform an honour of state. There was no word of what became of her parents. And that, we all thought, boded ill for them.)

On this particular day, it was a Diktat. I listened, as usual, with my ears on stalks, tracking the sense of it through the ponderous phrases: '...the high achievements of our educators...such have been the great steps...no further need for study...greater use elsewhere...report to the work commissar at five tomorrow morning'.

The teacher sank to his seat as if winded. His face was a picture of unease. With no top classes to teach, how would he keep his job? How would he feed his family?

Alyosha turned to me. 'Work commissar? Five in the morning tomorrow? What does it all mean?'

There were schoolmates all around, and no one knew now who could be trusted. So it seemed sensible to say no more than what the Diktat had, but in plainer words.

'We're dismissed from school,' I explained. 'It seems our teachers have done such a great job with us that there's no point in holding us back any longer from helping fulfil the Great Economic Plan.'

He stared. 'Leave school? At *twelve*?' He seemed delighted. 'Who'd believe our luck? Escaping from this place two whole years early.'

'Almost three for me,' crowed Misha behind him. He turned to the boy at his side. 'What will you choose to do, Vasily? Will you drive a train? Or go to be a sailor?'

Dreamers! The very next morning my mother shook me awake at four. 'Yuri. Get up!' There was no fire. To warm me, all she could offer was some cold radish stew she'd kept back from my meagre supper.

I forced it down and staggered out into the icy dark street.

I'm not sure what I expected. Could I have been enough of a fool to think the work commissar would be standing there at Depot 157 with a list of our strengths? 'Dmitri, your teachers tell me that you sing like a thrush. Off with you to train at the opera house! Georgio, you're strong, so you can be a woodsman. As for you, clever Yuri, it would be criminal not to take advantage of your skills with the pen. So you can choose: will you write films to cheer and encourage the workers? Or would you prefer to sit in an office and write something more serious – reports on the logging achievements along the eastern boundaries, perhaps? Or an account of power station construction?'

We gathered in the yard, some of us half asleep still, some jumping with excitement. The work commissar glanced at the sheet of paper in his hand, then all he said was: 'Names starting with A to L to the cement yard. As for the rest of you, you're to be hod carriers.'

Alyosha turned to me. He looked mystified. 'My name begins with M. So does yours. Medev. Molovotz.'

Too sick to speak, I nodded.

He was staring. 'Hod carriers? You and me? The cleverest boys in the class?' The blood drained from his face and he said it again. 'Hod carriers!'

We'd seen them often enough, on building sites and bare terrain cleared for some new purpose. They stumbled over the rough ground, their faces swathed against the wind and sleet with filthy rags. Their backs seemed permanently bent and, even in their thick mittens, their hands looked like claws.

I heard a voice behind us. 'What about me?' It was poor crippled Vladimir. 'Am I supposed to swing a hod along with me between my crutches?'

The idea was such nonsense, we showed no sympathy. Vladimir, at least, would have to be found some other job. But his complaint just seemed to highlight the fact that Alyosha and I both had firm legs and strong backs. And if a country's goal is Equality for All, who can complain when letters of the alphabet are taken to double as dice to determine people's futures?

A cement yard's no picnic place. Could hod carrying be any worse?

CHAPTER FIVE

Now came what, in my stupidity, I took to be the worst time of my life. Each morning I was shaken awake before dawn, to hear myself whine like a baby.

'I can't! Too cold! Too tired!'

Sometimes my mother was gentle. Sometimes her irritation showed itself. 'On your feet, Yuri! Do you want us all to suffer when they come looking for you?' Either way, I'd try to push down bitterness. No point in asking how it had come about that she had the good fortune to work in the warmth of a press of bodies and machines, while I was forced to work outside in even the worst of weathers.

Shivering with cold, I'd stuff down the only few mouthfuls of food I'd have till noon, and follow my mother down the crumbling concrete stairs to our block entrance.

Here we would part. She'd give me a quick hug of sympathy and hurry off to her factory. Then I'd tramp off down the street.

Most days, at one of the corners I'd meet Alyosha.

Ruefully we'd shrug at one another and fall in step. Sometimes we grumbled about the unfairnesses of the day before. Mostly we picked our way around the potholes in the road in gloomy silence till we reached our place of work – a building site right at the edge of the town where vast new blocks of flats were being built in a hurry to house the families pouring in from the country. ('They come to join the Next Step Forward,' we were told; but their lost faces and stick-thin arms and legs told quite a different story of why they'd abandoned their villages.)

At five, the foreman swung open the doors to his store hut to herd us inside and stand watching as each of us picked up a hod. In some the wood was rotten. Others rattled from loose joints. But not a single hod could ever be declared beyond use.

'This one's a goner,' the last boy to push his way into the storeroom would plead with the foreman.

'It's worked till now.'

'But the back's soft from rot! It's half off. One more load of bricks will finish it.'

The foreman would scowl with irritation. 'Stop your slacking, boy, and get those bricks up there. The men are waiting.'

Sometimes you'd be lucky. The man you'd been paired with would be working at ground level, and you could take your bricks to him carrying the hod at such an angle as to put less strain on its rotten side. More often there would be no choice, and you would have to climb the shaking ladders, dangerously fixed almost above one another so, if you slipped, your bricks would fall so closely past the boy struggling up beneath that he'd be showered in grit. Even if you were the only one on the ladders, you'd hold your breath and move gingerly, rocking the hod as little as possible for fear that any moment you'd hear the creak of splitting wood, and feel that sudden lightening of your load that threw you so off balance that you might tumble after your falling bricks.

Then you would have to work for three whole days without wages to pay for a new hod. 'Unfair! It wasn't me who broke it. It was rotten to the core. Why should I pay for it?'

The buckets in which the mortar was raised were in no better state. But still it seemed a rule that in the Land of Freedom all equipment was perfect. Breakages or collapses must be due either to care-lessness or to deliberate sabotage. So I soon learned to hold my tongue and, at the end of the day, lay any good hod or bucket I'd come across on the side furthest from the stove. Next morning, when we stumbled in, the softest boys would rush for a place near the stove's open doors, and make great play of sorting through whatever lay on the floor around them while they soaked up warmth. I trained myself to be sterner, and spent the time rooting for whichever hod and bucket I'd taken care to hide the night before under some frozen rags in some dark corner.

In any case, what could a few minutes within sight of two or three short lengths of burning wood do to set up a body that faced whole hours in the biting wind? Some days it was too cold for even the brickies to work. The mortar we raised up to them on the frayed ropes froze in the buckets before they could reach over the sections of wall they were building to haul it in. On days like these we might be sent scouring for wood. We'd wander off down unpaved tracks into the straggling fringe of forest still waiting to be cleared, and think ourselves in heaven because we were gathering sticks like feeble old men.

The spring drew on so slowly. Then summer came at last. At noon they fed us well. Sometimes the soup even had a few stringy threads of meat in it, and I grew taller.

'See, Yuri? Hard work suits you,' my mother teased, though she was as disappointed as me that, before I was even thirteen years old, my life had drifted into this long hard street that had no end. Sometimes she'd reach across the table and turn my hands over, weeping on the scars and callouses. 'And you still a boy!' was all she dared murmur, even to me. But I could see the words behind her eyes. Shame! Waste! Disgrace!

Then came the day of the accident. As usual I had forced my way to the front of the rush to the store-room, snatched up my halfway reasonable hod, and set off to the stacks of bricks beside the wall. The brickies didn't thank you for bringing them the chipped and broken ones, so even here there was another jostling for the best.

At last I set off with my load: sixteen bricks firmly settled on my shoulder, packed in the hod four by four. The workman I was fetching for that day was called Big Karl. He came from the east, and hardly ever spoke. If you were ahead with the stacking, he might nod as if to say, 'Well done.' If you fell behind, you'd find him waiting, fists on hips, scowling. The look on his face alone would be enough to make you tip your bricks out in a rush and scurry down the ladders for more without taking even a moment to catch your breath.

That morning I was on the highest ladder when I heard – a floor or so beneath – that soft cracking sound that meant a hod was collapsing, followed at once by the sound of bricks sliding and the usual yell.

'Watch out below! Watch out!'

Did the unlucky boy make the mistake of trying to hold his bricks back by twisting the hod round? In any case, it was too late. All that he managed to do was point his falling load even more truly at the boy climbing the ladder below him.

Beneath me, I heard a desperate scuffling noise. The ladder groaned. There was a scream cut off by a pitiful thud.

Did Karl see the blood drain from my face? Instantly he dropped his trowel to lean over and lift the hod from my shoulder as easily as if I'd been carrying feathers.

Free of the weight, I dared look down.

'Alyosha!'

I was back down the ladders in no time at all. But he was dead. Spread on his broken back, staring up wide-eyed, a look of shock still on his face.

'Alyosha!' I buried my face in the grit on his jacket. 'Alyosha! Alyosha!'

The foreman pulled me off, but not roughly. Now I was crying my eyes out. 'Alyosha! Alyosha!'

Somebody led me away, back to the storeroom,

and left me to weep for a while. Then, at a word, I had to dry my tears and pick up my hod. Alyosha's body had vanished. Though people were making detours round the place where he'd been lying, everyone was working again. I filled my hod and lugged it up the ladders. When I reached the top, Big Karl stopped trowelling for a moment to turn and speak.

'A friend?'

'We started school together.'

He nodded. 'Bad luck. Bad luck indeed.'

Then he went back to his work.

Again that word. Luck. As if there were nothing that couldn't have been predicted about ladders set too close together and hods so rotten they were bound to spill bricks. Hours later, as we sat round, dispirited and silent, eating our soup, I heard myself saying it.

'There should be rules about such things. The state of the hods and the buckets. The jammed pulleys and the fraying ropes. The safety of the ladders. There shouldn't be such careless accidents. Someone should see to it, and straight away.'

'A brilliant idea!' scoffed Vasily. 'We could make fine rules for ourselves. No more than four bricks in a hod, I say.'

'No more than eight hours' work a day!' said someone else, raising another laugh among those to whom
Alyosha was no more than a face that had vanished.

'Why stop there?' Anton said. 'Why not a rule that
we can't work at all when it's too cold?'

'You'd only need inspectors to go round checking.'

'Inspectors! Yes!'

They fell about laughing. I knew I was doing what
Grandmother always called 'talking my head off my
body'. But I couldn't leave it. Somewhere, a few
streets away, the boy who'd made a thousand ice
slides with me, laughed at my jokes and whispered
answers when I was stuck in class was lying dead on
some slab.

'What's so crazy about the idea?' I persisted. 'Don't
they make rules for us already? Rules about everything. A rule that we can't take our tools home at
night, not even to repair them or keep them safe. A
rule that you have to wait for the whistle outside in
the freezing cold, not in the warm storeroom. A rule
that we have to stay after hours whenever the
foreman demands it.' I spread my hands. 'So what
would be so odd about a rule to keep the ladders
further apart, to stop an accident even an idiot could
have foreseen?'

I'd gone too far. Nobody spoke. They stared

uneasily down into their bowls of soup. Finally Caspar said boldly, 'Father Trofim said each of us was to think of ourselves as a small spoke in one of the wheels carrying the Great Revolution as far and as fast as it can go. He warned us the path will run through rough ground and some of the wheels may get damaged. He says the only important thing is that the Revolution keeps rolling on.'

I had a vision of lanky blond Nikolai back at Pioneer camp. He hadn't said one word that could be proved to smack of rebellion; but with one beatific smile he had managed to make it clear exactly what he thought of sending volunteers to battle without boots or guns.

With poor dead Alyosha in mind, I wanted to speak up as well. But I am not so clever. The smile I tried to summon must have appeared no more than a cold sneer. The only words I managed to spit out were, 'Ah, yes! Of course! The Revolution! Rolling on towards our Glorious Future!' And any fool listening would have been able to hear the disbelief in my voice.

The whistle blew to get us back to work. I scrambled to my feet and was the first to pack my hod with bricks and get to the ladders. All afternoon I worked like a fury, hauling the bricks up to the top floor at such a rate that I was soon piling them higher than the strip of wall Big Karl was working on.

At the end of the day he clapped a hand on my shoulder. 'You've lost a friend, Yuri. Still, there's no need to work for two.'

It was the first time he'd touched me – or even called me by name. I felt the tears rise. Shyly I glanced up to catch him looking at me in the way my mother looked at my hands – as if to say, How can this be happening to someone before they've even had the time to grow into a man?

CHAPTER SIX

'Alyosha?' My mother gripped the cloth wrapped across her chest. 'Little Alyosha?' She sank onto the stool. 'Oh, the black grief of it! His poor, poor mother!'

Grandmother merely shrugged. I turned away. When I looked back, I caught her eyeing my torn boots and guessed she was already wondering if she dared go round and, under the pretence of offering our family's condolences, beg for the use of Alyosha's for herself or me.

But no one dared answer their door now – not even at the saddest times. And Alyosha's sister would need the boots soon enough. So, clearly shaking off the thought, she muttered only, 'One poor soul lifted from the road of bones,' and settled back to scraping the last of the crust out of the bread pan.

My father was last home. I watched him shiver when he heard. 'An evil day!' Each time he passed behind, I felt his hand on my shoulder, as if he needed to assure himself that this boy hunched over the table, still trying to stem his tears, was at least warm to the touch, not lying cold and still like his poor friend.

It was a comfort. Next day I felt calmer. The sun shone silver through the breaks in the cloud and I fell into the rhythm of work almost with pleasure. At noon we sat eating our soup as usual and, though no one mentioned Alyosha, I felt that I was being looked at with sympathy by my companions. When I dropped my crust of black bread into the gap between us, Georgio even passed it back instead of snatching it up and stuffing it into his own mouth.

So I had nothing in mind when, just as dusk was beginning to fall, I heard shouts and a rattling. I reached the top of the highest and shakiest ladder before I dared turn. But once I was safely over the parapet of bricks Karl had been laying, and onto the firm concrete base, I took the chance to peer down.

The noise was coming from the gates. Two men were shaking the chain, and shouting at the foreman to let them in.

He'd seen their uniforms. He hurried over faster than he'd run to Alyosha on the ground. He tried to undo the padlock in such haste he twice dropped the key and had to scrabble for it in the little heaps of spilled cement around his boots. The minute the chain ends fell apart, the men stepped into the workyard.

Just for a moment the three of them stood talking, the sunlight glinting on the silver badges on the guards' caps. Then, as the foreman turned with a finger stretched to point, I felt Karl's hand on me for the second time within twenty-four hours. He was pushing me down behind his freshly laid bricks.

'It's you they're after.'

'*Me?*'

'Aren't you the one who opened his mouth too wide over his soup?'

'All I said was—'

He cut me off. 'Whatever you said, it was more than enough.' Still holding my head down, he was pulling me over the rough cement floor to the other side of the building, alongside the trees.

'Quick!' he said. 'Get your foot in the bucket.'

'In the bucket?' I peered over the edge. What was he thinking? To lower me over like a load of mortar being sent back down?

I thought he was mad and my face must have shown it.

'Use your wits, Yuri. Either you risk a fall now, or you wait for those men to make even more of a mess of you later, here or in their cells.'

'Cells?'

'Yuri, wake up! You've seen the colour of their uniforms. You know who's coming for you.'

And if I was pale before, now I was grey with fright. I knew the men must already be striding across the yard towards our block, kicking aside anything that lay in their path, as they'd soon be kicking me. Suddenly I felt I could smell, even from so far up, the leather of their holsters and the oil in their guns. I would be dragged away without a chance. I'd heard enough about the Leader's guards to know that either I'd never be seen again or, if I did come back, people would take one look at what was left of me and think the men in grey would have been kinder to finish the job properly while they still had me.

'Yuri!'

This time I jumped to it. I held out my arms, and Big Karl lifted me, as if I were a child, onto the parapet. I jammed my foot in the bucket so hard it felt as if I'd cracked half the small bones. Karl fed me a short length of rope and closed my hands round it with his own iron grip. He tipped the bucket. It slid off the parapet with a scraping noise I felt must alert the whole world to what was happening on our side of the half-built block.

Almost at once the bucket fell away, with me swaying dangerously, out in thin air.

I clung, sick with fright, as Karl began to lower me. The bucket rocked. I shut my eyes in terror. Surely I must weigh more than a bucket of mortar. Surely the rope would snap and, like Alyosha, I'd go hurtling to the ground.

The bucket fell in sickening jerks. Desperate to know how fast we were descending, I forced myself to open my eyes. Karl must have been letting me down hand over hand, controlled and steady at his end, jerk and sway at mine. My hands were slick with sweat, but somehow I kept my fingers round the rope even through desperate cramps. Each time the rope caught, a juddering pain ran through the foot jammed in the bucket.

Down and down I went. Karl was lowering me at one of the places along the building's shell where there were no gaps for windows so I had no fear of being seen. Behind me were the bushes and trees we'd scoured for firewood on days too cold to get the mortar, unfrozen, to the men. At least I knew the paths. And now the trees were in leaf, I might at least stand a chance of getting away without being spotted.

From the top of the building I heard an angry

shout. Karl's voice. 'Yuri! Damn you, boy! Yuri! Where are you? Get up here with those bricks! I'm waiting!'

If he was trying to fool the guards, they must be close now.

Just at that moment the bucket started sliding at such a rate, it was like falling. Were the guards at the top of the ladders? Now I knew Karl must be letting the last of the rope run through his palms, burning his skin.

I hit the ground.

'Bricks here! Bricks, I say!' I heard Karl roar to cover the noise my bucket made as it rolled down the slope to the bushes. The rope slithered down to land in a heap at my side. Clearly Karl thought it less risky to throw the last of it over in case they pulled up the bucket and guessed how he'd helped me.

Praying for his sake that neither of the guards knew enough about building work to think it strange Karl had only the smallest heap of mortar at his side for all the bricks he was shouting for, I gathered up as much of an armful of the rope as I could carry, and ran for cover.

Once I was hidden, I snaked the rope end towards me, keeping my eye on the parapet for fear that either of the men hunting me should take it into his head to peer over. As soon as I'd hauled the last of it out of sight, I crept a little further down the bushy slope, and left the bucket lying on its side, the rope trailing after, so even if Karl didn't get to it first, he would at least be able to argue it had fallen off the parapet and rolled away.

'That's why I sent him down again out of turn,' he would be able to tell them when they questioned him. 'To fetch back the bucket the young fool knocked off my wall.'

I stumbled off between the bushes and trees, desperate to convince myself Karl wouldn't find himself in the worst trouble. And only then, as terror from the dreadful, swaying descent began to fade, did I remember that things could go as badly for me if I were found.

Or even worse.

I speeded up till I'd outrun the furthest paths we'd ever searched for firewood. It was getting dark. More out of breath than I had ever been, I finally slowed my pace, telling myself that going more slowly was sensible. Suppose someone who'd been working in the wood suddenly appeared on the path? Surely they'd think a panting, rasping boy far more suspicious than one who was simply strolling along and whistling idly.

I pursed my lips. I'd no intention of making any

noise at all unless I met a stranger. But even without trying I knew that any attempt to whistle would end in failure. My mouth was parched from fright. I hurried on. And it was only as the relentless thumping of my own heartbeat in my chest and ears gradually calmed that the realization came to me.

I was in even deeper trouble than I feared.

How could I go forward? I had nothing with me. No food, no money, no identification papers. Nothing except the rough and ready work clothes in which I stood.

And I could definitely not go back.

So I went on. What I had taken to be the silence of the woods turned into almost a comfort of rustlings and flutterings and strange short screeches in the night. What would my mother be thinking? Would the guards think that she and my father were lying when she assured them I had not come home? I felt a sickening in my gut. Perhaps they'd even arrest my parents in my place – we knew it happened – and keep them down in their slimy basement cells in the hope that I'd present myself at their gatehouse the same way young Victor went in search of his brother in Grandmother's story.

Grandmother! Surely the soldiers wouldn't drag

her away! She was a wily old bird, well capable of making herself look even older than she was, and acting half-witted. Perhaps she'd have the sense to whimper and drool, and leave them thinking her brain so full of holes and worms she might as well be left.

At heart, though, I knew that neither my grandmother's age nor my parents' innocence would be any protection. If they chose to, the guards would beat them. We knew they'd thrashed confessions out of peasants accused of hiding grain, and wreckers and saboteurs. For years my parents had struggled to convince themselves, 'They must have been guilty of *something*. No one's arrested for no reason at all.' But after the day my mother came home with the news that Simple Talia down the street had been taken away in one of their Black Marias, even that small fraying effort at self-comfort was snatched away. ('If they're accusing dafties like her, soon they'll be coming after planks of wood.')

The only words ringing in my ears now as I tramped along the forest paths were those from Father Trofim's endless speeches: 'There will be sacrifices. In the interests of the greater good, small mistakes may even be made. But better one or two innocents are temporarily troubled than that the guilty escape.'

I'd listened. I even recall the scorn that ran through me when I heard the bland words 'temporarily troubled'. (By then we all knew very well what sort of 'trouble' his guards would offer with their steel-capped boots.) I'd even thought back to Nikolai in Pioneer camp, and paid more attention to the Black Marias passing in the street and the scraps of torn posters in the gutters. But I'd still pushed it all from my mind, thinking it had no bearing on my family. In any case, work was so punishing I no longer had the energy to care about anything over and above my own next meal and the next chance to sleep.

Now, for the very first time, I realized truly what his words could mean. It was the job of the guards to make sure nothing and no one stood in the way of the Revolution. It didn't matter how old or frail you were, or how unlikely it was that you were hiding something or weren't telling the truth. If there was any chance at all you might be lying, it had become their 'duty' to beat truth out of you. After all, hadn't Father Trofim said it often enough? 'A stick of any sort can stop a wheel. All must be broken.'

I pushed my way on and on. In places the under-growth was now so thick I had to kick and beat the branches away. In others, the rutted path was wide enough for two. My poor, poor parents! What had I done? How could it be that the stupid outspokenness of one person in a family could lead to the punishment of others? How could they drag my mother away by the hair because her boy had said a few unguarded words? What sort of person could pile such terror onto someone who'd just lost her only son without the chance to hand him his one warm coat, or say goodbye?

Up came the moon at last. Now I was cold, and hungrier than ever, but I could at least make faster progress and have more confidence I wasn't wasting time by wandering round in circles. It struck me suddenly how very strange it seemed to be by myself. All of my life I'd either been with my family, or in a class or a squad, a march or a parade, a team or a troop. Always in groups. Always herded, with people watching every move and listening to every word. It seemed so odd to be, for the first time in my life, striking out alone. I was just thinking how, in other circumstances, walking between these whispering trees would be a great adventure, when suddenly the moonlight that had been filtering meanly through the branches above washed over me in a flood.

The trees had given way to bushes. Within a step or two even the bushes opened up in front of me, and I was tripping over metal track.

The railway line.

Here, at least, was a choice. So far as I could tell, this had to be the track between our town and Xhosa, half a day along the line. Should I make for the city?

Or would I be safer hiding in the forest? I'd heard of others who had managed to stay alive through the summer months, living off any small animals they could snare, and nuts and berries.

I stood at the side of the track. Part of me longed to turn round and creep home, hoping against hope there were no traps around our flat, no men with silver badges on their caps waiting inside, lounging against the shutters and smoking their cigarettes as they watched the street and waited for the stupid boy they guessed would soon run out of courage and come crawling back to his mother.

But to leave our province entirely! That was too much of a decision. I wasn't ready. Perhaps I'd be bold enough to think about it the next day. But not right then.

And then it struck me. Within an hour or two, they would be after me with dogs. No use to tell myself that I was small fry – some silly boy not worth their time and effort. They already knew how little I'd said, and still they'd bothered to come after me.

Now I'd defied them, they'd come after me again.

I was just wondering how fast the news of a runaway boy without papers could pass from one telegraph post to the next when, under my foot, the rail stirred into life.

It was my only chance.

I had to take it. So I jumped the train.

CHAPTER SEVEN

Jumping was scarcely the word. The goods train that steamed into view a few seconds after I stepped back into the shadow of the bushes was going so slowly that I could all but step onto one of the footplates. I knew it wouldn't be long before the track ran past some woodsman's cottage, or over a crossing where, in the moonlight, I might be clearly seen. So I inched my way, spreadeagled, along the train's side, clinging to every hook and handle, until I reached the wide expanse of a sliding door.

I listened for a moment. No sound came from inside, so I tugged at the handle. The door glided open easily enough. Apart from a couple of broken crates, there was nothing on the floor. But on a rack along one edge lay heaps of empty grain sacks.

Perfect covering! Swinging myself onto the rack, I pulled a sack up to my waist and tugged another down over my head. Worming my way into the heap, I stretched out to wait. Twenty minutes was all I needed. Half an hour at most. Any dogs they sent after me would lose the scent at the trackside. The guards might wire their warnings up and down the line, but just so long as I kept clear of stations, I had a chance of staying ahead.

I lay, half-choked with grain chaff. The gritty feel of it bit into my skin. Stifling sneezes, I counted the minutes in my head. I wanted the train to carry me a good few miles further from the city, but it was important not to risk falling asleep and being found on board at the next halt.

Was it the rhythm of the counting or the clack of wheels over the joints in the rail that dulled my sense of purpose? In any event I woke to the sound of a bored shout. 'Xhosa! Xhosa Junction!'

I'd slept for hours. Daylight was speckling through the sacking. Cautiously I peered through its coarse weave. My heart thumped fit to burst, but apart from the shaft of light streaming in, nothing had changed, and there was nothing to be done except hope no one outside had noticed that one of the truck doors was no longer shut.

It seemed an age before, with a great jolt, the train moved again. I let out the breath I'd been holding, and almost at once heard the sound of boots and voices. Startled, I turned my head to see that what I'd taken in the dark to be a truck cut off from all the rest had narrow sliding doors at either end.

Every last muscle tensed again as I listened. First came a laugh. Then: 'Mischa! What a story!'

'Oh, I could tell you a score.'

'Finish this one, if you please.'

'Where was I? Oh, yes. So this brand new little heroine of the Motherland turns out to be no more than eight years old, with the braids in her hair pulled back so tightly that her face is all but scraped back into them.'

I heard a fiddling with the latch as the man kept on with his story. 'The winsome little thing comes up to the Leader and curtseys. And he smiles down at her, and even gets out of his chair to take her hand and walk her round the statue of herself. Of course, she's far too over-awed even to speak, so he tries to put her at her ease. "Don't it look just like you?" he says to her. "Down to the Medal of Honour!" '

The voice broke off. I heard a series of grunts. Then, as I watched through the sacking, the door finally juddered along its warped runnel just enough to let a grizzled man in soldier's uniform wriggle through into the truck.

The other man followed. 'He's good with kids, you have to give him that.'

His uniform might have been different, but their lined faces were so similar, each might have been the other's reflection. The two of them glanced around the truck before the taller one called Mischa went on with his story.

'So the little girl simpers and curtseys some more till the old man gets bored and shows it. His guards can't rush in fast enough to sweep the kid back to her foster mother. And even before our little heroine Yelena is out of the door, he's turned to Plotov, and guess what he says?'

'What?'

'You won't believe this, after all the fuss about her up and down the country. He says: "To think of it! Denouncing her very own parents. What a little turd!" '

The second man tugged the door safely closed behind the two of them before he said, 'Takes one to know one!'

Both of them laughed. I knew they must be talking of Father Trofim as surely as I knew they must be brothers. Only two people who trusted one another with their lives would have dared share a laugh at that last remark – and only then when, as in this truck, they thought there was no chance of being overheard.

I watched as they strode across to tug at the next door.

'Jammed tight.'

'Here. Let me.'

But even with the two of them putting their shoulders to it, the next door wouldn't slide.

'Damn!' The shorter one turned. 'No chance of getting through. We may as well work our way back to the others.'

But the other had lowered himself onto a crate. His voice was serious. 'Tell me first, Maxim. What's it been like up here?'

'With the peasants?' His brother brushed a couple of filthy rags off another of the crates before he settled. 'A strange sort of farming indeed! The peasants have no grain, and so we harvest them instead, and send them off to prison camps.'

'That bad?'

'Worse.' Maxim leaned forward to slide the side doors further apart. Forest had given way to open land, and we were travelling faster. 'Look, Mischa. Didn't they tell us in school that this part of the province was called the Bread Basket? Do you remember?' He waved a hand. 'And look what's happened. No drought. No crop disease. But still there's famine everywhere. The smallest children are arrested for stealing ears of corn or pinching apples. A farmer's machine breaks down and he gets twenty years for wrecking.' He spread his hands. 'Why would a man wreck his own machine when already he can't feed his family, and is so desperate he's ripped the straw from his own roof to feed the last of his beasts?'

For a while neither spoke. They simply stared at the countryside as it rolled past. Then Maxim turned back to his brother. 'See? The fields are choked with weeds. The harvests have gone from "not enough" to "nothing at all". Last year the commissariat took most of the peasants' fields "for the public good". Now this year, to punish them for not producing crops they won't get to eat in fields they no longer own, each peasant has even had his own last little family plot cut back to nothing.'

He pulled his crate closer to his brother to say more softly: 'Mischa, last week I drove through one village where every single family had had their land cut back to their very cottage walls.'

'Are they to *starve*?'

'Yes. Both as a punishment and as a warning to other villages.'

'His orders, of course?'

'Oh, yes. His orders.'

Mischa spat. 'Always his orders! The man has his fingers in every pie. Why, he must never sleep! *And* he has spies all around.' He snorted with contempt. 'Oh, how the rest of them must regret easing him to power! They might have known *who* he was, but never in a thousand years could they have guessed *what* he was.' Mischa's voice brimmed with scorn. 'And now it's far too late for even that pack of jackals to change their minds. He's polishing them off, one by one. He's finished bothering with all those "heart attacks" and "accidents". One word out of place now and you're in the cells, having the stuffing kicked out of you till you "confess".'

Again the two of them fell silent. And it's hard to explain, but hearing these brothers talk was stirring my heart inside me. How long had it been since I'd heard anybody speak his mind? So long, I'd forgotten. I might have been cowering in dirty sacks, covered in wheat chaff, but hearing these brothers talk to one another so candidly was like stepping out of a cage into fresh air and birdsong. I looked back at the life I'd been forced to abandon and realized it was years since anyone I knew had spoken so freely around me – even my grandmother. My parents' gathering fears had even put a curb on that brave tongue. Oh, she might still have said a scathing word or two from time to time about the old Czar. But dare to mention Father Trofim? Not in as long as I could remember.

Maxim was leaning closer to his brother now and taking care to speak even more softly.

'I'll tell you this, Mischa. I think this Glorious Leader of ours has come to think you're the better man for showing no mercy. Either he truly believes these starveling peasants still have stockings filled with gold coins, or . . .'

'Or—?'

'Or he's waging war on his own countrymen. Think of it! He divides their land time and again to give more and more of it to the commissariat. If they object, he sweeps them off to prison camps up north – whole families, Mischa! Down to the youngest child! He gives their farms to strangers. He's taken their crops, their cattle – even the last of their few chickens. He's broken the countryside – turned it into a desert – and now that there's barely a grain of wheat growing there, he's happy to arrest the whole lot of them out of revenge and spite.'

The voice fell to a whisper. 'Think back to what we learned in school. You know as well as I do that if the Czar had treated even a dozen of his serfs this way—'

'Oh, yes! The country would have boiled over! And yet this madman's sunk his teeth so deep in us that thousands go missing and it's as if he tips their bodies into water. Within a moment, silence closes over them. Nothing is said.'

'Even by those around him?'

Mischa spat again. 'Brutes.'

'*All* of them?'

'Every last one. Yesterday I heard a story. Father Trofim loses his favourite fountain pen. A few days later, one of his henchmen asks him, "Have you found it yet?" and Father Trofim answers cheerfully, "Yes. It was under the sofa." Instantly the head of security leaps to his feet. "I'm sorry, Leader, that's impossible! Down in my cells I already have a dozen who've confessed to taking it." ' Mischa shifted uneasily. 'Last week I heard—'

But he broke off. There was a thud of footfalls getting closer. Before the brothers even had time to pull their crates further apart, there was a rattling and the door they'd come through slid back on its runnel.

The soldier who pushed his head through asked, amiably enough, 'Is some conspiracy afoot? Look at the pair of you, sitting like two old ladies at the parish pump.'

Maxim waved an idle arm towards the open truck side. 'Just admiring the view.'

The newcomer glanced out. 'What's to see? Nothing but forest again now.'

Unruffled, Maxim added, 'And I was telling Mischa here of all the women he'll miss now he's insisting on leaving that soft city berth of his to go back to a fighting batallion.'

The interloper grinned. 'Isn't this a week's leave? Your brother must make the most of his chances.' He jerked a thumb towards the passing countryside. 'From what I've heard, it doesn't take much to make a peasant woman lift her skirts round here. I'm told a quarter of a loaf will do it these days.'

Mischa rose. 'We'll come with you. Time for a turn or two at cards before we reach Strevsky?'

Strevsky! My heart nearly stopped again. In the next province!

The crates were kicked aside. The brothers brushed the grain dust off the back of one another's trousers. And then all three of them were gone.

Less than a minute afterwards, I was gone too. The moment their footsteps faded, I was bolt upright, pulling off the sacks. They'd left the side door gaping wide. I leaned out only long enough to peer ahead and check the steepness of the slope beside the track.

Then, even before the train began to slow for the long rise to Strevsky, I'd hurled myself out, head first like a circus tumbler, somersaulting over and over, down the long slope and into the trackside bushes underneath the trees.

CHAPTER EIGHT

So was it good fortune or bad that sent me rolling down the slope into that patch of wild strawberries? Because sometimes when I look back I think that, without their cheerful little red faces spread over the ground to offer a glimmer of comfort, I might have given up on the forest right there and then, and set off along the track to almost certain arrest as I neared the next station.

Instead, with my mouth and hands stuffed with berries, I took off between the trees. A little further along I came to a clearing with hazelnuts for the picking to replace the few berries left in my hands. Cracking them between my teeth, I ate enough to satisfy the last of my hunger, and still kept on, stuffing my pockets till hazelnuts spilled out of them.

Then I pushed deeper into the forest.

The ground was soft with moss. Lichens climbed the tall silver birches, and everything around me breathed out scent. I couldn't help but think that, if I'd not come here in this way, leaving behind all I had, I would have been so happy picking my way between the trees, choosing this path over that, upstream over downstream, this cloudberry over that bilberry. If I'd not been a boy in a province not his own, without his papers, I would have sung from sheer good spirits as I walked.

Each time the path divided, I peered down both ways. When it was dry, I chose the path on which sunlight speckled most strongly. After each shower, I'd take the one along which the raindrops clinging to the branches shone brightest silver.

I walked all day, drinking from streams and napping on beds of emerald moss in dappled clearings. Even my worries about my family gradually settled. After all, everyone knew I'd run from the building site, and not from home. A few sharp questions here, a man watching the door for a week or so, then, just as the guards would have to face the fact that I'd slipped out of their grasp, so surely my parents would be able to comfort themselves I'd got away safely.

They would have trust in me.

It seemed so easy to spread a comforting gloss over what I'd left behind. I felt as if I'd stepped into a whole new life, a world away from the drab city and the grim building site where I'd been working. I walked through dusk, and into the night. Now, when I looked down two paths, I'd pick the one the moon lit best because it was easier to pick out the writhing tree roots that tried to trip me.

Time passed. Paths narrowed to nothing – little more than the sense that someone had trodden here before. I found myself meandering this way and that. What little of the moon I could still see kept slipping behind cloud. The forest here seemed blacker, and the squawks and rustlings from all the creatures around seemed to get louder and become more threatening.

Whoomph! Out of nowhere came a blow. It hit me in the stomach, winding me so hard I fell.

I heard a scuffle and a rustling. The moon slid out to light a bent old man, as gnarled and skinny as the stick with which he still threatened me. Hard to believe this ailing greybeard had dealt me such a blow and was clearly so ready to give me another.

The voice came out as a snarl. 'Who are you? Why are you creeping around here so late at night?'

I rubbed my belly, fighting for breath to answer before the stick came down again. And maybe because this was the only day in my whole life when I'd been free to choose my own paths and go my own way, I found myself – since I had nothing honest to tell him – falling back on the answer of the schoolroom.

'I've been sent.'

'Sent?' He peered as though mystified. 'Sent? Who by?'

Still on my knees under the threat of his stick, I found that my wits were sharpened. I offered the only answer that might allay his suspicion that I was some runaway.

'Sent by the commissar.'

His face constricted from fright. He dropped the stick as if it scorched him, leaving me sure that, had I been daft enough to say anything else, he would have used it again and again, till he had beaten me to a pulp and so been rid of me.

But it was as if the very word 'commissar' had defeated him. He waited warily while I pulled myself to my feet. I stood like a foolish block of wood, and in the end, clearly at a loss himself, he muttered, 'Then I suppose you'd better follow.'

I reached for the stick he'd tossed aside so fast. In the strange silver half-light I saw a tremor run down the scraggy lines of his face. He watched me heft the stick's weight from one hand to the other, and only after I'd offered it back did I realize that, in his eyes, I was a dangerously fit young man, not some fraught lad scared to be travelling without permission or papers in the wrong province, and trained in good manners by a grandmother as old as himself.

I fell in behind him on the narrow path. Soon we stepped out of the shadows into a flood of watery moonlight falling on a patch of cleared land. To one side, deep in the shadow of the woods, was a cottage so tumbledown it looked as if it had already sunk half into the earth.

A few feet into the clearing, the old man stopped and turned. His eyes were glittering. Then, as if some festering bitterness had fuelled a burst of courage he didn't even know he had, he pointed with his stick.

'So there he is! The boy you've no doubt come to chase, lying as idly as your commissar suspected. Feel free to dig him up and drag him back.'

For a moment I was baffled. Then, looking where he pointed, I saw a long thin heap of freshly tossed earth.

Somebody's grave.

Not knowing what to say, I waited. Perhaps I stood so still I looked like one more shadow, for suddenly, hobbling towards us from the broken-backed cottage, came a sparrow of a woman as old as the man at my side.

Her voice was quavering. 'Pavel?'

I took her to be speaking to her husband, but as she came closer it was clear that her eyes were set on me. 'Pavel?' It was a note of disbelief. 'Can it be you?'

The moment she made out my face, the strange look of hope on her own snapped into one of suspicion. Pulling the old man close, she hissed in his ear, 'Who's this? Why is he here?'

The old man whispered a warning. 'Take care! The boy comes from the commissar.'

She turned to face me. Now moonlight picked out her eyes as clearly as I'd just seen his. But where the old man's had been gleaming with tears, the glitter in hers was born of hatred and scorn.

'Sent by the commissar? Why? To see if you can find yet another way to make a misery of the last of our wretched lives? Isn't it enough to herd my family onto a train going heaven knows where, and leave their poor boy broken-hearted?'

The old man clutched her arm. 'Maria! Curb your tongue.'

She shook him off and pointed to the grave. 'There he lies!' she snarled. 'Go back and tell that butchering commissar of yours he killed my grandson when he arrested his mother. Go tell that murdering thief that the very last thing left to us is safe from him now. Safe underground!'

The old man was still trying to hush her. 'Maria! Enough! Each word you say will be reported back.'

She turned her fury on him. 'What's left to lose? They've stolen our land and taken the last of our grain. We've no seeds to sow, no fields to sow them in. We've nothing now but what's around us. Igor, you know as well as I do that when the snows come we'll be dead within a week – frozen or starved.'

She spat on the ground. 'So why should I worry what I say in front of whichever little worm the commissar has sent to torment us?' She turned her scornful look back on me. 'A boy so stupid he must have lost the path a dozen times to show up at this time of night!'

But what sharp eyes hunger must give. The woman had no lantern. Only the moonlight shone on me. But still she'd noticed.

'Grain! You have *grain*?'

I glanced down. Sure enough, not all the chaff from the sacks had blown off my work jacket.

Pushing his wife aside, the old man gripped my arm. 'What? Have you brought back some part of what you took?'

I couldn't bear it. I'd thought that we were hungry in the city. I'd heard the soldiers talking on the train, but hadn't truly realized things could be so much worse.

I hung my head. 'I've a few hazelnuts in my pocket.'

Again the old woman spat. But Igor asked, strangely gently, as if, now the damage was done, he was simply curious, 'So why were you sent?'

I gazed across the clearing at the pitiful hovel in which these two old scarecrows were scratching through the last of their days. The roof was sadly buckled and full of holes. Weeds straggled at my feet. I thought of the forest cottages my grandmother had told me about in her stories – homes that could stand firm against the worst of winter snows, with crocks filled to bursting: pickled lemons and cabbages, mushrooms and onions and plums; barrels of salted melons, pears in vinegar, soused apples; and loaves of rye bread sitting on every shelf.

What had the old woman said? 'Dead within a week – frozen or starved.'

I was no good at hunting. So:

'I've come to help you fix the roof,' I said.

CHAPTER NINE

Those were strange days. I knew the two of them would have found it a good deal easier simply to hate me. But I was young, and worked hard. Each morning the old man came with me into the forest and showed me which trees to fell – not so young they wouldn't bear the weight of the brushwood we'd soon be spreading over them, but not so thick I couldn't drag their stripped trunks back through the forest.

He did his best to help. He tried so hard, I even teased him: 'Igor, you'd strength enough to bring me down with that old stick of yours. How come you can't replace your own rotten roof struts?'

He growled at me, 'Wait till your own bones crumble. Then you'll not need to ask such half-witted questions.'

Most of the time, though, he stayed silent. Silent and sour. I longed to ask him whether all the terrible things I'd heard on the train could really be true. But, like his wife, he treated me with deep suspicion, fearing that anything he let drop would be reported back.

I even wondered if I should confess to him. A dozen times or more I thought of putting down the axe and saying, 'Listen, there's no need to keep your beak so tightly buttoned in front of me. I wasn't sent by the commissar. I lied in fright. I'm just a runaway with no papers, wondering how to get word to my family and trying to work up the courage to move on.'

But I kept silent. After all, Maria might have snapped, 'Why should I worry what I say? What's left to lose?' But once she learned I'd stumbled on their hovel purely by accident, she might think differently. Simple enough to creep up on a boy while he slept, stave in his head and hide his body in a ditch to keep him from blurting out secrets.

I knew I couldn't stay. But surely the more I could learn about what was going on in the countryside around me, the better I'd be able to fool the curious later about where I was going, and why.

It wasn't easy, though. The pair of them stubbornly pretended never to hear, or understand, my questions. I think they thought that, even to have stayed, I must have somehow discounted their first strong outburst at the commissar – perhaps put it down to grief. From the moment he handed me my first dipper of water and she pointed out the heap of sacks that was to be my bed, it was as if they were starting afresh with me, as careful and as guarded as anyone else.

But I was patient. I think I guessed that, like my grandmother, these two had lived for far too long through times when people were free to say exactly what they wanted. They couldn't play this silent game for ever.

And I was right. For as I gradually won their good-will by doing all the things they couldn't manage, their guard did begin to slip.

Tiredness helped. All day they'd act like two old prisoners in some dank cell who thought it wiser always to speak blandly or well of the jailor. Darkness would gather round the wretched cottage, and suddenly, even without prompting, I'd find that one or the other was freely spilling out a stream of bile about the miseries of their existence.

One night in particular, Maria lost patience – first with me, then with discretion. All day she'd been complaining about the pains in her legs. She'd snapped at me when I rose, and when I was going out into the forest, and when I came back again.

At supper time she handed me the usual bowl. The swirling mess inside gave off a smell so rank I held it further away.

'So what's in this? Stewed rat?'

'Next time, bring grain with you,' she told me sourly. 'Then I'll bake bread.'

'Eat it,' said Igor calmly. 'Some days we think ourselves lucky to be sucking the meat off bats' wings. So while there's anything at all in your bowl, have the good sense to work your jaws harder than your eyes.'

I stirred the ghastly broth. The bones that swirled in it were needle-thin. I lifted up the spoon, and with it came a stinking moth-grey lump. 'Is it some crow you found lying in the clearing, dead from old age?'

Maria snapped, 'If you'd prefer fat roasted wood-pigeon, catch it yourself. Soon we'll be chewing sweat out of old rags.' She saw my shudder. 'Oh, yes!' she scoffed. 'What would you know of hunger, little commissar's boy? My grandfather stayed alive through one bad winter scraping out the hooves of his starved horse, then chewing on the horn.'

But feeling so ravenous had made me outspoken. I pushed the bowl away. 'I've worked all day. Do you think I can stay alive on slop like this?' I braved an echo of the two brothers in uniform I'd overheard on the train. 'There's been no drought round here. No crop disease, either. Surely there must be wheat somewhere in this province. Or is it that famine is now made by *man*?'

Before her husband could frown her out of saying it, the old woman spat her answer. 'Yes, when whole villages are stripped of all they grow!'

She'd gone too far. The old man covered his ears with crippled old hands as if he hoped there might still be some chance that I'd go back and tell the commissar, 'That good man Igor refused to listen to his wife's treachery.'

I had to seize the moment – while she was sitting rubbing her swollen legs and couldn't care. Leaning forward, I whispered, 'There must be some reason things have gone this way.'

She gave me a look of contempt. 'The day those bullies of yours start bothering with reasons, be sure to let us know.'

I wanted to tell her right there and then that they weren't *my* bullies. No, not mine at all. But all I dared say was, 'All this misery can't stem from *nothing*. The villagers must surely have—'

'What?' Behind their sagging hoods, her old eyes flashed. 'Showed the commissar their starveling children? Reminded him that you need land and seed to fill a wheat quota? Told him that when a machine is starved of oil, it'll stop working quite as reliably as if "wreckers" have been at it.' She spat. 'In short, been desperate enough to speak up against the new rules!'

I spread my hands. 'How does it *happen*? How do they *let* it happen? How can whole villages full of people allow themselves be tormented by so *few*?'

She stared at me as if I must have stepped off the moon to know so little. 'You're young,' she said at last. 'You're green and stupid.'

She dropped her head until I could no longer see the scorn in her eyes. She rubbed her legs again. It was a while before my sharp ears caught the last few words she muttered:

'And you have yet to learn that, when he goes stalking, it never troubles the wolf how many the sheep may be.'

That night I dreamed of Nikolai. I saw him standing on the barricades, his cap perched jauntily on the side of his head, holding his flag high and taunting the men in uniform standing in ranks fifty paces in front of him, waiting for the order to charge.

'Join us!' he bellowed. 'You know you're on the wrong side. Weren't you all workers and peasants before you were forced to be soldiers? The future lies with us! With justice and fair shares and liberty for all. Break ranks and join us!'

I woke, my heart bursting with pride. This was my friend! I could still feel the bite of the spring wind on my cheeks and taste the smoke of the street fires.

And then it struck me. The street in my dream came from the history book in school. That was the Gortov bridge. There were the tramlines. The cap Nikolai wore was the sort we had worn all our lives in school parades and off at Pioneer camp. The banner he waved was our old banner.

In my head, Nikolai stood for those with courage enough to try to shake off this brute who'd seized the seat of power and set about throttling our country. Yellow and black. But in my dream he had been waving the flag of those we'd learned to praise: those first few brave young leaders who'd had the strength and vision to overthrow Grandmother's old Czar and start the Glorious Revolution my mother once truly believed would rid the world of corruption and start things afresh.

With justice and fair shares and liberty for all!

So there it was. The years roll by. Governments come and go. Everything changes. And everything stays the same.

So Grandmother had been right each time she said it, after all. 'Only a fool cheers when the new prince rises.'

CHAPTER TEN

'Tell me about Pavel,' I begged next day, when Igor and I were dragging the last of the birch trees back to the clearing.

Perhaps he thought his wife had spoken her mind. Why hide things now? Maybe the fact that within a day or two he'd have a better roof over his head went some way to softening him. Maybe he simply wanted to talk about a grandson he'd loved.

Whatever the reason, instead of apeing deafness the old man answered. 'Never a strong boy. From birth, he'd fall in fits and thrash on the ground.' His face went dark. 'But after your men had—'

'Not *my* men,' I interrupted firmly. 'I keep on telling you. I was *sent.*'

He let the matter go. 'Well, to be fair Pavel was soft in the head all his life.' He peered between the trees, as if to check his wife wasn't there to listen. 'Maria won't have it, of course, but I believe things might have been easier if he'd been dragged to the train along with all the rest of them.'

'*All* the rest?'

He gave me a wary look, then shrugged. Again I had the feeling he thought the damage was already done. He might as well tell me the story.

'They took the whole village – all that were left, of course. The men and grown boys had been taken for soldiers more than a year before.' Dropping his end of the birch spar, he stared off between the trees as if he were watching things as they happened. 'First they herded the women out of the fields and pushed them into trucks. Then the guards seized all the old folk who had come hurrying up to curse and wail at them as they carried off their daughters. They swept up the children still clinging to their grandmothers' skirts.' He spat on the ground. 'And after that fine work, they went back for those still sitting in the dirt, too young to walk.'

I busied myself pulling the birch trunk along by myself as he trailed after me, passing his sleeve over wet eyes. It was a while before I dared bring him back to his story. 'But you and Maria . . .?'

'We'd left already.' He sighed. 'We're old enough to know one straw's enough to show which way the wind blows. First your fine commissar stole our last cow with that long fancy word of his.' The venom Igor felt had clearly oiled his memory.

' "Requisitioned". Yes, Butterpat was "requisitioned".'

He spat again, as if the very word had soiled his mouth.

'Then that great swaggering thief sent men in uniform to "redistribute" our share of the communal grain. But I can see as far into a stone as any man, so when they came back for the last of our chickens—' He broke off. By now we were in the clearing. As if suddenly thinking better of his frankness, he wrapped up the story. 'So Maria and I threw the last few things we had into the barrow, and pushed it back here.'

We stacked the birch strut with the others and went back for the brushwood. As soon as we were a fair way from the cottage, I started my questions again. 'How far away is this village?'

'A day and night of walking.'

'So how did you know about this place?'

He gave me a wry look. 'Come, lad. A man is born with legs, not roots. My father built it. He was a woodcutter in this very forest.'

'How did you get to hear about what happened back where you came from?'

He let out a sour laugh. 'Everyone knows it's a very foolish goose who comes to the fox's sermon! Those in the furthest fields had the good sense to hide when they spotted the dust of the trucks coming down the hill from Strevsky.'

'Was Pavel one of them?'

'Poor Pavel hadn't wits to hide. Most likely, when the screaming started, his eyes rolled back and he fell into one of his lathers of writhing and drooling. None of the soldiers would have wanted to drag him to the truck. They would have feared he had some fever.'

'So they just left him there?'

'Alone. Not fit to feed himself. Barely able to walk.' Old Igor kicked at the brushwood he was dragging as it snagged in a bramble. 'Of course the news crept back. "Just one young daftie left," we heard. "Keening and shivering and falling on the ground." We knew it must be Pavel, so we went off to fetch him.' Igor looked at me with something close to pride. 'That long walk, mind. And with Maria's bad legs. *And* pushing the barrow, to fetch the boy back home.'

He tugged his brushwood easily over a stump. 'See?' he said. 'I've taught you well. You felled that tree cleanly.'

'Get on with the story,' I told him, little thinking the skills he'd taught me would save my life a short while later.

'There's little more to tell. We skirted village after village on the way to get Pavel. All empty.'

'*All* of them?'

'All of them. Everyone gone. "Cleared from sheer spite," said Maria. And when we got there, it was just as they'd told us. The boy was squatting in a doorway, mumbling and shaking. We wrapped sacks round him and gathered his last few things. And though we hadn't enough food to keep ourselves, we brought him back with us.'

I wondered what the 'last few things' of someone like Pavel might be. I knew the old man kept a tattered Bible deep in his mattress. I'd seen him pull it out when he thought I was asleep, and heard his wife's fierce whispers: 'Igor! Put it away! Better to be arrested for stealing food than reading about angels so blind they can't even see when a country's bleeding to death!'

But surely Pavel couldn't read. And though old folk might cling to hidden Bibles, no one my age had ever been given pictures of saints, or crosses on a chain. What would a boy like him keep? Not coins, for sure. They'd have been taken from him to pay for food. His papers? Certainly. Perhaps a few pretty stones and lumps of glass he'd picked up playing in the village dirt, and fought to keep. Maybe even a photograph. I knew from Grandmother that some of the peasants had stood for the camera back in the old days, when there was still time for fairs and holidays.

I had the heavier load. Hefting the wayward layers back on top of one another, I stumbled after Igor as he tugged his own fan of brushwood over the roots and stumps, and kept on with his story.

'On the way home, we heard a whisper that the villagers had been packed onto a train going north.'

I thought of the great frozen bay. 'Up to Kolskaya?'

'To work in the mines, we heard. Nobody said the name. All I heard was that, all the long winter, not so much as a rim of sun rises above the horizon. The days are as black as the nights. And, in the summer, the sun never sets.'

'White nights . . .' I murmured.

We both slowed our pace. The dusk was gathering. I don't know what Igor was thinking. But I was remembering Grandmother. Suddenly I saw her in my mind's eye, as clear as paint, cursing the feeble fire beneath her blackened pots and talking of those condemned to count out year after year with the blows of their axes. My mother too. 'Lucky to come back at all,' she'd always muttered. The comfort I'd created for myself slithered away. Now, for the first time, I faced it honestly – the thought of being severed for ever from my own family; the fear of what might have happened – still be happening – to them; and, even if the worst had failed to happen, the horror of knowing they might be crawling through their days and lying wide awake at night, sickened with fear about what might be happening to me.

Now I understood why Igor said it might have been better if Pavel had gone with the others. It would be easier for his mother, surely, to know at least whether her son was living or dead.

'What happened?' I asked Igor to distract myself. 'Why did Pavel die?'

'I say his poor heart broke. With his mother not there to soothe him, he fell sick in a different way. He lay on those same sacks as you, and lost the feeling for life. And as he got weaker, it was as if those terrible fits of his lost interest in tormenting him.'

I waited while Igor sniffed back tears. After a moment he told me briskly, 'But his end was peaceful enough. The last few days he simply lay staring up at the sky through the holes in the roof. There was none of his usual mumbling and keening. And a boy who had always pushed everyone else aside to get to his food could no longer be tempted by even the freshest of hens' egg—'

He broke off and shot me a furtive glance.

'Couldn't even be tempted by *what*?' I said. 'That brushwood of yours is making such a noise I can't hear what you're saying.'

'Nothing,' he said.

And, knowing we'd each of us lied as clumsily as the other, we worked in silence till the darkness fell.

That night every muscle ached, but I couldn't sleep for thinking of the boy who'd lain on the filthy damp rags under me only a short time before, staring up at the sky through the decrepit roof.

Tomorrow the holes would be gone. I'd build a makeshift ladder with sturdy lengths of wood and a heap of knotted twine Igor had dragged from some corner. We'd pull off the rotten struts. I'd haul the new ones up and lay them close enough to one another that, once the brushwood had been spread across, the holes could be stopped with handfuls of straw packed down with clumps of moss.

With luck and a better roof to shelter them, the old man and his wife might last a little longer. But Pavel was gone. Life had drained out of him on these very sacks. The night I came, I had dropped onto them without a thought except that they made a softer bed than the earth-packed floor. But now I realized that, since that sad soul had been lifted out of them, they'd probably not even been shaken.

I was lying on another boy's deathbed.

It was enough to keep sleep well away. I thought of slipping out under the stars until I'd shaken off my grisly imaginings. But the old man had worked all day at my side. I didn't want to disturb him.

That's how I came to be awake still when I heard the rustle – not just the usual restless stirring from the old couple, but more as if someone were feeling around for something on the floor.

I made great play of rolling over in sleep, then watched from behind a flung arm as the old woman pulled herself up and, painfully slowly, tugged on her boots. Again I thought of my grandmother. With three flights of stairs to stumble down and a court-yard to cross, she'd had to reach for the night pot. All Maria had to do was shuffle over to that little patch of bushes they'd pointed out to me on my first day.

I watched through the gap she left in the doorway. But in the soft dawn light I saw her go another way entirely – along the only path Igor had never led me along in search of good trees to fell.

Curious, I waited. It seemed an age before I saw her hobbling into view again, holding her hands in front of her, palms upward.

And resting on them?

Hens' eggs.

She'd kept them well enough hidden while I was spooning up her radish stews and those strange patties I could swear were filled with nothing more than roots and grubs.

Is cunning like fever? Can you catch it from the people around you? Next morning, as the two of them were pulling on their boots, I sat bolt upright and said, 'Do you hear a hen?'

I tipped my head to make a show of listening. 'Yes! A hen. And getting closer.' I pointed one way. 'Down that path.' Then I pointed another. 'No! Down there.'

Of course they heard nothing. There was nothing to hear. But knowing that my ears were young and theirs were old, they took my word for it. Nothing was said, but in an instant the two of them were out of the cottage, one heading down one path, one down the other in search of the hens they feared must have escaped from their pen. Hens they were determined to keep secret – so secret they'd let me starve rather than share a single egg.

In an instant I'd rolled off my rags. I pulled the sacks off the mattress on which the old man lay. Sure enough, there was the hole. I spread my fingers wide, but in there was only the greasy old Bible.

Throwing the sacks back, I scrambled to my feet. Where would a sharp old woman hide eggs from the boy who'd worked his fingers raw bringing spars for her roof? She'd not trust them to foxes outside.

There were no cupboards. All the shelves were bare. The floor was hard-packed earth.

And then I saw the shoes under a broken stool. The strips of ancient leather were stretched across a netting of braided birch bark, with a stuffing of hay.

A stuffing of hay. And inside each of them, a fresh hen's egg. Other things too. In one, my fingers touched a fat round coin. I pulled it out. Gold!

And in the other, a piece of folded paper.

I unwrapped it carefully. It was the papers of Pavel Tretsov. Of Strevsky Province. Age fourteen.

I was no thief. I pushed the gold coin safely back in the hay of the shoe and pushed the eggs in after as carefully as if I'd laid them myself.

But I put Pavel's papers in my pocket.

That night I nagged and nagged until Maria agreed to lend me the stump of her pencil and a scrap of wrapping 'to write a letter to my mother'.

'Three lines at most, mind! It won't last for ever.'

I wrote the lines. Next day I worked without a break, fixing the roof spars, spreading the brushwood over, then clotting every last hole with moss and earth.

That night, as soon as both of them were snoring, I dropped the pencilled note where they would see it when they rose.

I was not sent by the commissar. That was a lie. I'm on the run. I know your secret, but you'll soon guess mine. So let's trust one another.

And even before Maria had risen to look for her eggs, I was gone.

Chapter Eleven

The size of our country! Five days I travelled – mostly to be quite sure that no one would look at my papers, then at my face, and know they weren't a match. And still I found myself beneath the Chelya hills, barely a step through that great province.

Seen from a train window, the countryside I walked through, mostly by night, no doubt looked normal enough. But to a boy scavenging along the way, it was as if a host of locusts had passed through. Where had the rabbits gone? Had even the ptarmigans starved? Around me was nothing – nothing! One night I had the good luck to stumble over someone's dying fire while I was carrying a stinking crow I'd not been able to bring myself to eat, or toss aside.

It was a risk. Maybe whoever built the fire was still close by. Nevertheless, I sneaked out of the darkness and flipped a couple of embers onto a scoop of bark torn from a rotting stump. I crept off. Further along the path, I stopped to listen. Everything seemed silent enough. So I pushed my way deeper between the trees and scraped around for dried leaves and twigs for kindling.

That crow! Who'd have believed it seemed to me a feast – the sort of meal a prince might call for in a fairy tale. Next day I found some moulding pignuts and a few more roots, and, hours later, stumbled on a clearing with berry bushes. All stripped bare.

By the fifth night, the dizzy spells were getting stronger. With my knees trembling so much that I could barely walk, I came upon the outskirts of a village. It seemed the only choice left to me now was between courage and starvation.

I plumped for courage and crept closer.

Someone was sitting, idly whittling wood in the moonlight, on the step of a huge wooden hut. Even from where I stood I smelled the stench. For just a moment my starved brain thought the foul reek must come from the man I took to be some sort of night guard, as if his body were rotting from the inside out.

But then I realized. It was poultry droppings!

If this was a chicken hut, then this must be one of the communal farms. I drew back into the shadows of the straggling woods and waited till dawn, hatching my plans and practising my story – even the words in which I'd tell it. Just as the night was thinning into grey, I thrashed as noisily as I could through the last bushes, whistling cheerily, and, walking up to the step, confronted the dozy guard with a confident greeting.

'What ho, comrade! Pavel Tretsov. Sent to help clean out the chicken house. Have I come to the right place?'

Would it sound mad to say that was the happiest time of my whole life? My arms were pecked till they bled. I had to learn how to force my way through masses of frenzied chickens happy to kill one another and me for a beakful more grain. I learned how to chop off their heads, and how to hoist a sack of feed onto my back, and how to carry the vast trays of eggs without breaking a single one.

I learned how best to scrape muck off the floors and how to recognize sickness in birds, infections in the eye, and combs that paled and drooped beyond the general misery of being stuck in a shed with no fresh air or grasses. Sometimes at night, when they'd all laid aside their endless brawling and screeching, and perched on their crossbars with their pitiful wilted combs, I'd think of them as prisoners trapped in a sunless jail – creatures to pity.

Except that they didn't have to go to Study Circle. Lucky hens!

Study Circle was *misery*. We were a model communal farm, it seemed. Twice a week we all traipsed down to the nearby village hall to listen to a heap of ranting and barking about what we should believe. A joy for those who cared about whether This Disgraced Leader had only gone awry when he said That, or That Disgraced Leader had already become a traitor when he said This. But for a boy who'd spent the day shovelling chicken shit onto a compost heap and carrying buckets of water to the troughs through piles of demented hens, it was a torment.

And a danger too.

I should have known. I should have paid attention. After all, I was eating better than ever before in my life. Nobody knows how many eggs a hutful of hens has laid each day until they're counted; and once you've learned the knack of throwing a raw egg down your throat and crushing the shell in the muck under your boots, you grow strong fast.

I'd even managed to send word home. I cadged a stamp off friendly, amiable Galina, and had the sense to address the letter to Alyosha's family, not mine. '*Everything's fine here,*' I wrote in letters as plain as print – nothing like my own. '*But please go round and tell Uncle Grigor and Aunt Lily that their precious parcel arrived here safely.*'

I knew they'd pass the hidden message on. So for the first time since I ran away, I could at least be sure I'd done my best to stop my family – if they were still alive – worrying about me. All that I had to do was keep my wits about me in the endless meetings. But with the shortage of oil, none of the lamps was ever lit. It was so easy to close your eyes against the drone '. . . cost of production . . . fluctuations of supply . . . means of subsistence . . . sectarianism . . . instruments of labour . . .'

Usually I'd come to my senses at the Exhortations. Or, at the very least, at the Denunciations. We all pinned back our ears for those. After all, that was the way you learned how things had tightened up since the last meeting, and just how careful you now had to be.

Often, on the walk home, you'd get an even keener sense of how the land lay. 'Where was Galina tonight? I didn't see her in her usual place. Could she be sick?'

There'd be the most uneasy silence till someone dared say it: 'The guards came suddenly and took her back with them.'

Again, the silence. We'd all heard Galina muttering to herself over and over about the fact that there
were no longer matches to be found. 'How am I
supposed to light the oil heaters without them?
What if the hens die of cold? I'll be blamed quickly
enough for that.'

But nobody knew who might have told on her.
And so the only safe thing to say was, 'She must have
done *something*.'

And maybe some of them truly believed she must
have done something more than grumble about one
of the shortcomings of the New Rational Agricultural
Method. But, either way, it was important for all of
us to say the words out loud, with people around to
hear us. We'd all heard the tale of innocent little
Sofia, who'd worked on a neighbouring farm. She'd
been invited to a party. She'd never had a drink
before and one of the men had managed to convince
her it was 'a tonic'. While she was puking up her guts
out in the yard, one of the boys had said something
scathing about Father Trofim.

Sofia wasn't in the hut. She didn't even hear it. But
still, one or two days after the first wave of arrests,
the guards came back to get her. The other dairy
maids had heard her pleading as she was dragged
into the Black Maria. 'How could I "hush up"

something I didn't even *hear*?' Yet with the new Non-denunciation Laws, claiming that you didn't know what had been said was no excuse. The only safe thing was to stay away from people whose tongues were too long.

And away from idiots like me, the night I sent my life careering off the rails a second time.

Oh, I heard the question the lecturer asked me. 'Who was the first man to recognize that there had been deliberate sabotage in the rail system and take steps to rid the industry of the malign influence of wreckers?' Indeed, I was busy amusing myself with my usual pastime – translating the question into plain language: 'Who lost his temper and hanged half the country's precious engineers because a lack of investment had led to delays and breakdowns?'

A child would have known to offer the answer, 'Good Father Trofim.' (Even if that were wrong, and just for once somebody else was in the line for praise, I could be sure the lecturer wouldn't correct me for fear of falling foul of yet another new offence on the statute book: 'Robbing the State's Principal Strategist of His Due'.)

But, from the bench behind, I heard a firm whisper. 'Palchinsky! Palchinsky!'

Later, I learned that someone was putting out his

hand for a rag to stop a draught. He said 'Palchinsky' only to wake his neighbour to the need to pass it across.

But, like a fool, I spoke out, brave and bold: 'Palchinsky!'

How was I to know the dozing man's namesake was a famous wrecker? (And he himself was lucky. Now that people were being arrested simply for living under the same roof as the accused, there would be scores in cells from the mere accident of sharing a blackened name.)

'Palchinsky?'

The shock round the room was palpable. My brain, half stewed all day in fumes of chicken shit, instantly cleared as I realized what I'd done. How can your life be capsized by a whisper? Already the women sitting on either side of me were inching away. There was a scuffle at the door as if, for their own safety, some of those standing there were already elbowing one another out of the way, to be the first to denounce me.

I sat there thinking of what someone had said as we watched poor Galina's children rounded up to be swept off to the state orphanage.

'This morning they were a family. Now there is nothing. Everything is gone for ever.'

Not daring to mix with such a dangerous babbler, I'd fallen back at once, pretending not to hear.

And by the time I rose to leave that hall, believe me, everyone had done the same to me.

Everyone had vanished.

CHAPTER TWELVE

The room was enormous. Above the stove hung the usual vast portrait of Father Trofim. Along two sides, bookshelves were stacked floor to ceiling with box files. The rest of the walls were plastered with posters showing men with steel mittens crushing others in their grasp, or vipers with men's faces being poked from their filthy nests.

All around me were the shrill and twisted slogans we'd been taught to shout in the mass rallies and torchlight parades. 'Root out the treacherous crow-bait!' 'Blood for blood.' 'No mercy!' 'We must break the enemy's wings.'

The bottom halves of the windows were thickly smeared with paint. Above my head a naked light-bulb hung, and round the room dangled flypapers thick with the bodies of flies and bluebottles – some dusty and desiccated, some still oily bright or busily struggling.

Beside me stood two guards. They had the dread badge on their caps – that vicious silver serpent, coiled to strike. They'd booted me around so much I'd no brains left to listen. I stared up at Father Trofim's hard painted eyes as the inspector read out the final charges.

'Provocateur ... Propaganda ... Agitation ... Panic-monger ...'

Did the man sitting so calmly at his desk realize how absurd it was, what he was saying of me?

'*Panic*-monger?'

One of the guards stepped closer, as though to kick me some more. Lazily the inspector waved him back. My head dropped in my hands. I had explained a hundred times. There was no point in persisting.

Nonetheless, I was stunned by just how quickly and easily the sentence was pronounced.

'Ten years' hard labour.'

'Ten *years*?'

But even as the words came out of my mouth, I realized I'd feared worse. We'd all known eating an apple could count as 'Theft of State Property'. We knew the weak and old and simple-minded were being dragged in under the blanket accusation of 'Limiting National Progress'. But the recent decree on Revealing State Secrets had caught out a dozen people from our communal farm before we'd grasped the fact that anything they chose could count as a secret now. All talk of epidemics. Mention of a local airport. Discussion of the harvest. Why, simply saying the word 'famine' could earn you twenty-five years.

Ten years was almost nothing. It was a sentence for a juvenile. Over the last few years we'd watched Father Trofim take against Mongols and Jews, Yakuts and Kazaks. Some of the new countries inside our ever-widening borders had all but been emptied as every man or woman who dared raise a voice against the banning of their folk songs – or even of the growing of their national flower – was packed onto a punishment train. You'd think the mineral mines up north would now be bursting at the seams, but for the rumours that grim conditions chewed up the lives of prisoners so fast, even the daily spill-outs from the trains could scarcely keep pace.

It would have happened soon enough, I thought: arrest for something – it barely mattered what. My luck had lasted longer than expected. Even in this dull, faraway province, the squalid roll call was turning into a billowing flood.

I was one fleck of spume on one small wave of it.

I scarcely cared. 'Thank you,' I even heard myself saying as I was dragged to my feet and bundled out of the room to make space for the next. I suppose I thought that I'd be thrown back into that slimy dark hole where I'd spent the last few days. (Three? Four? The beatings and interrogations had followed on one another's heels so fast I'd lost all track of time.)

But no. Instead of kicking me down the stone steps as usual, the guard pushed me past the arch into the glare of a long corridor studded with doors. Unlocking one at the end, he shoved me in, over a heap of legs stretched out on the floor.

A wave of grumbling met me. 'Take more care!'

'Keep your damn boots to yourself!'

'Hush up, there. Settle down.'

Somebody pointed to the corner in which a bucket leaked in stinking pools onto the floor.

'I can't sit there.'

'Then stand.'

Within a minute the mass of bodies had settled back to how they were when I came stumbling in. I leaned against the wall, realizing with a fearful drop in spirits that, just as my entrance into the cell meant nothing to anyone in it, so my disappearance from the life outside meant nothing to anyone either. As easily as those on the communal farm had accepted that I'd been 'sent', so they'd accept that I would not come back. Already I could hear the whisper with which they would distance themselves from any more thought on the matter. 'Pavel? A shame. He seemed a nice enough boy. But he must have done *something.*'

Such was the power of Father Trofim. After all, everyone knew Galina was good and loyal. They had no reason to think worse of me. But still I knew that almost all of them would find it easier to think that she and I (and all the hundreds of thousands of others) had betrayed Father Trofim, rather than risk for a moment daring to think that things were the other way round: that *he* had betrayed *us.*

And I admit I didn't feel that my life was over. (Maybe I was too young.) Deep down, I still believed that somebody – soon – would take the trouble to review my case and listen to my story. I couldn't for a moment really believe that I had been shunted, like some old railway truck, into the dead-end siding of quite the wrong life. Indeed, after the storm of beatings, there was a strange sort of tranquillity about the cell, as if the very stones of its walls were telling me, 'For now, the worst has happened. Leave anguish to others. It's safe to shut your eyes.'

So, in fits and starts, I slept.

By morning the seat of my trousers was stuck to the floor. The stench from the bucket was making me, and those around me, retch. Each time one of the other prisoners came over to add to the overflowing pail in one way or the other I struggled manfully to get further away, but found myself firmly held in place by the press of bodies around me.

Forty-two men in a cell with bed boards for six.

No. Forty-five. Three darkened heaps I'd taken to be bundles of possessions suddenly stirred into life.

'How many new in the night?'

'Just the boy.'

They all knew where to look. The one who'd asked the question spoke directly to me. 'Yes, yes. It's not a dream. Everything around you is real.'

Someone else asked, 'Sentenced?'

'Ten years,' I told them in tones of deep self-pity, and was astonished to find my words greeted with incredulity and laughter.

'Ten years!'

'Ten!'

A young man with scrubbing-brush hair and freckles over his broad face was staring at me with envy. 'Only *ten*?'

'It's a boy's sentence,' someone beside him explained.

He gave me a scowl so deep that you'd have thought I chose my own sentence. 'Lucky to be so wet behind the ears,' he growled. 'Ten years indeed!' He caught my stare. 'Yes! Look me in the eye! I'm given twenty-five for "having an underground weapons arsenal". Know what that means?'

I shook my head.

'It means that when they turned the ridges of our cabbage patch, they found some rusty old knife.' He groaned. 'Twenty-five years! All of us! Mother, sisters – everyone!'

Beside him on the bunk, a gaunt-faced man said, almost conversationally, 'Once, if a man were given such a sentence, the crowds would gather. There'd be solemn robes, drum-rolls and declarations.'

'Tell us, Professor,' someone said scornfully. 'How would that make things better?'

The gaunt man bridled. 'It showed that, back in those much despised days of the Czar, a man's life at least *mattered*.'

There was a thoughtful silence. Finally someone I couldn't see said idly, 'Twenty-five years . . . Now it's as routine as getting a ticket for the bath-house.'

'Better than Tygor's sentence,' someone reminded him.

I couldn't help it. I was curious.

'So what is that?'

Everyone glanced at a man with a badly torn lip as if to offer him the chance to tell his own story. He simply shrugged, so one of the others answered in a tone of mock solemnity: 'Tygor's been sentenced to the "Supreme Measure".'

He'd picked the wrong way of saying it. Tygor's indifference snapped. 'Leave out their mealy-mouthed fudging! Do me the honour of calling my sentence by its real name.'

Shocked to be staring into the face of a man with no future, I failed to guard my tongue. 'What?' I said. '*Death?*'

'A smart boy!' someone sneered. 'And I see from the scabs on his face that he's already learned that the word "persuasion" means being kicked around the cell till blood spurts out of your ears.'

There was another burst of laughter. And suddenly my spirits rose. I looked at these men – sweating and filthy, some of them wearing rags, and half of them old enough to be my own father – and I felt comfort. It was as if a trapdoor had been flung open above my head. Before, I'd only seen a few slim shafts of truth filtering down between boards. Now, suddenly, plain-speaking flooded in like noonday light. What did it matter that I was sitting by a stinking bucket if, every time one of these men opened his mouth, I learned so much about the world around me? Another man would be thrown in. Another, like Tygor, pulled out. And each would have his story – even if those still in the cell turned out to be the only ones to learn its end.

Tygor never came back. When, three days later, word was tapped through the walls about his fate, one of the men said idly: 'To think our only epitaph will be the letter.'

I raised my head from chasing lice. 'What letter?'

He grinned. 'The one to the family. "This prisoner has lost the right to send or receive correspondence." '

I felt a jolt of shock. 'That means you're dead?'

'What else?'

The solemn man the rest of them had taken to calling the 'True Believer' spoke up as usual. 'It is the duty of those in power to put a stop to disaffection. That way, things will go better for the state.'

There'd been the usual wave of scorn. 'What, is Father Trofim listening behind the wall?'

'Save your prattle for your next party meeting.'

'Your own arrest was a mistake, of course! As soon as they realize what a loyal citizen you are, they'll send you back to your family.'

'Might even offer an apology. Why, Our Great Leader may go so far as to invite you for tea!'

True Believer scowled. The huge man at my side, whose wounds still wept from his last battering, tugged at my sleeve and nodded across the cell. 'Believe me, boy. That fool there's not the only monument to the power of Habits of Thought. You tell some men one great fat lie when they're still young, and they'll believe it all their lives. Nothing will shake them.'

He raised his voice at True Believer. 'Not even the evidence of their own eyes! Not even being dragged through a three-minute hearing instead of a proper trial, then dumped in this cage!'

I thought, with True Believer pretending not to hear, he'd let the matter drop. But, perhaps because of the pain of his wounds, perhaps through the anguish of worry about his family, the big man was working himself up into a fury. Now he was bellowing across the press of bodies: 'Admit it, cretin! You still believe all that fine tosh poured into your ears about Our Noble Leader. You still believe if the great man knew what was happening, everything would change! You really think that, don't you?'

Like some strange marionette, True Believer offered him only a blank face and yet another of those loyal remarks that seemed directed more at some microphone he thought might be hidden in the wall than at any real person. I was reminded how my parents had always said the safe thing in front of strangers. Did True Believer *really* still believe? Or did he secretly hope that one of the stool-pigeons put into every cell to snitch on others would bother to carry his words back: 'But there's a loyal man in cell nineteen. And we must let him go!'

By now, the man beside me had sunk back furiously into himself, spluttering and cursing.

An amiable-looking fellow called Boris tried to soothe things. 'What good would any trial have been to you anyway? Or any lawyer. What did poor Tygor tell us? The man they gave him was so scared for his own family that he scrambled to his feet and said in a nice clear voice: "The good of the Motherland is as dear to a defence lawyer as to anyone else. I confess myself as outraged as any other citizen by the defendant's crimes."'

All of them were remembering now. ' "The defendant's *crimes*"!'

'His own lawyer!'

'Lucky to get one, since they've become such a fast-vanishing luxury.'

'Twelve minutes, Tygor told us. That's all the time they spent, taking away a man's life.'

'Too many others standing in line outside.'

'Sittings all day and all night.'

Across the cell, a crooked man with a great burn mark down one side of his face spoke up for the very first time. 'Small wonder, given how things turn into crimes before you know it. Look at me! I had one single conversation with a friend about the fact that the streetlights had gone out again. She was arrested and beaten to a pulp. And what do *I* get? Twenty-five years, for "propaganda likely to dishearten the workers".'

The man beside him shrugged. 'At least you spoke! My daughter was thrown into prison just for having studied abroad. Was it her fault we came to blows with that particular country right at the time a letter was on its way to her old friends?'

Boris nodded at the one man in the cell who didn't seem to understand a word of any language tried. 'That poor sap didn't even go abroad. He just stayed where he was. The border changed around him, and he was arrested for not having a passport to the house he'd lived in his whole life.'

Everyone fell silent. Perhaps, like me, they were wondering how much greater a weight of bad luck there must be in the world, now sickness and famine and earthquake had been added to by men with pens, and pages to fill, in their books of new rules.

Certainly the next words spoken might have come from someone thinking along the same forlorn lines. 'I'm sure it made no difference. Bad luck would have come his way soon enough, now we're so busy spilling blood along so many of our borders.'

'One more excuse to tighten the knots a little more . . .'

'Tell them about the doctor, Boris!'

Boris lifted his head from picking fleas out of his shirt. Enough of us were looking his way for him to offer his story.

'In my last cell there was a doctor who'd made the mistake of standing beside a foreigner waiting for a tram. He couldn't for the life of him work out what the guards who arrested him were on about – "consorting with enemy aliens" – until they showed him the photograph they said proved his guilt!'

'Everyone in the whole province will be in here soon.'

'Except for the ones they lose!'

There was a roar of laughter. And after pitying my blank face, somebody triggered another round of merriment by telling me the story of Vasily Zemskaya, who froze to death in his cell, waiting for someone to find him and fetch him upstairs to the firing squad.

CHAPTER THIRTEEN

Eight days I was in that cell. When we were finally herded out at dead of night, I truly thought I'd been lucky. Only eight days! (Some had been stewing for months.) I hadn't yet realized that there are stages to despair – steps down through layers of misery until you reach a place where nothing – no, not even your own life – still seems to matter.

They pushed us out into the courtyard, where one of the first light snows of winter was beginning to fall. We sat like dogs at a gate and waited, shivering, until the guards were ready to move us through town.

We marched through back streets. 'In case the townsfolk realize just how many of us there are,' I heard someone mutter. And I could see how, if you happened to be looking out between your shutters and saw the wide snaking line of us shuffling along the streets in strictest silence, you might begin to wonder. All these men! Can these be the famous 'vermin' we've been told about so often, chewing at the roots of the state? But there are so many of them! And they look so much like us!

No, better to herd us round behind the glue factories and along the canal, though it must have taken a good hour longer to reach the station yard. It seems the women had been sent ahead, and were already bolted into their box cars. But how many cells had been emptied to furnish so many men? By the time we were pushed through the gate and followed the barked orders to squat in lines on the filthy boot-packed snow, I counted over four hundred.

And we were just the droppings from the prison of one small town! So how could anyone think we could be terrorists, wreckers, conspirators? If that were true, the Leader would have had to drown our revolt in blood, not simply usher us up ramps into the caged compartments of a train.

'Three more in this one! Quick! You with the arm sling. And you! And you!'

The guard grabbed at an old man stumbling up the ramp and pushed him so hard he fell into the carriage on top of me.

Instantly the old man was howling. 'My letter! Mind my letter!'

I lifted my sodden boot. The sheets of paper that

had slid out of his sleeve onto the board floor were already filthy and torn. The ink spread into pools.

'My letter!' His rheumy eyes filled. 'Now I must start again!' he wailed. 'Where will I find the paper?'

One of the prisoners crammed behind the closest mesh partition started to tease. 'Why bother, Grandpa? No one will ever read it.'

The old man held out the pulpy streaked mess he'd gathered from the floor. 'But it *explains*. All they have to do is take a moment to read it. Then they'll know I'm innocent. Innocent!'

His neighbours' snorts of contempt set him howling afresh. Beside me, the man with the arm sling broke off from shoving for a place, to offer a pitying look. I was the only one who heard the words he said so softly. 'Old man, forget it. The ideas of guilt and innocence died a long time ago. Now it's whatever keeps that wolf in power.'

But still the frail old fellow wept as he tried to sort his ruined sheets of paper. The other watched in growing irritation, then dropped his bundle to lay his one good arm round my shoulder and rebuke our snivelling companion: 'Be glad you've already had a life. If you're so keen to steep yourself in pity, feel some for the boy.'

The old man lifted his head just long enough to shoot me an angry look. 'No doubt he earned his place. But I am *innocent*.'

There was a round of jeering as men turned from fighting for space on the few wooden bunks or by the boarded windows.

'Does he have cloth for brains?'

'Oh, just our luck! Another True Believer!'

'Hey, Greybeard! Still trying to tug the glacier backwards?'

Even the one who'd put his arm round my shoulder couldn't help muttering, 'He must be some great professor. No man with ordinary brains could be so stupid.'

I turned away. I'd left a cell packed tight as herrings in a box only to find myself jammed in a place no better than a cage. Why hadn't I had the sense to take my chances while we were getting here? The moment I tasted the first snowflake and felt the fresh wind in my face, why hadn't I made a run for it? Stiff as I was, I might have made it. There had been rifles pointed at us, and at my first step out of line, more would have turned my way. But still I might have managed it. I might have dodged the bullets.

And then what? No one would open a door to a

stranger, no matter how desperately they rapped, or how much they pleaded. Since helping even those you didn't know were traitors had become a crime, no one would take that risk, especially at night.

No. Better alive than dead.

Feeling a jolt, I elbowed my way between the crush of men, ignoring their curses. If I stood tall, I could just see between the slats of a boarded window. Over the hills, the dawn was finally breaking. We were off.

Up to the north. New lands. No doubt they would be harsh. But there'd be clear fresh wind and, cold as it might turn out to be, surely there would be sunshine. Better than more time spent in that stinking hole. It was a crush now, certainly. But very soon, surely, surely . . .

I asked the man with the sling, 'How long will it be?'

'Till what?'

'Till we get where we're going. How long will the journey take?'

I was *excited*. I truly believe that – in my stupidity – I was keen to get there, keen to find new friends and maybe learn a trade. Even—

I heard his answer. 'Weeks. Maybe even months.'

'*Months?* Crushed in this carriage? In these wire pens?'

He gave me the look you'd give some foolish child. 'Believe me, you'll soon have space enough to stretch your legs. Sit by the weak, or sick, or old. There'll soon be room enough.'

Indeed there was.

There are enough who'll tell you about the transports: how we were beaten to pulp for making the slightest noise when the train stopped in a siding or a station. How we were fed on salted fish that blistered our lips, and turned us half mad from thirst. How we spent all our time chasing the lice up the seams of our rags and squashing them under our thumbnails only to feel their baby cousins already crawling in our body hair.

I'd prise one out of an armpit or my groin – even from one of my eyebrows. They might be flat and grey, they might be rusty red, swollen with blood. In either case, I got to love the sound they made when I burst them. The old train creaked along. We spent whole days in sidings – sometimes given water and sometimes not. Often, as we gasped with thirst, we'd hear the women further along the train set up a banshee commotion of howling and yelling. 'Water!

Be warned! We'll all of us scream till you fetch it! So bring us water! Water! Now!'

Admiring their courage, we'd set up a rebellion of our own, hurling ourselves against the wire sides of each compartment. All who were fit enough rushed, first one way, then the other. The sheer weight of our bodies could set our carriage rocking so hard the guards feared it would tip, and cause, not just our own, but all the other carriages along the train to topple off the track, like dominoes falling in turn.

'Water's coming!' they'd shout. 'Stop all that rocking or we'll take you out and shoot the lot of you! Water is coming!'

Sometimes the water came. Sometimes it didn't. And when it did, it always seemed that was the very moment the train jolted back to life and half the precious liquid slopped out of our bowls onto the carriage floor. We'd kneel to suck it up before it soaked away into the dirt and rough boards.

And every day – every single day – they came for the bodies. Sometimes it was only the old or the sick. (The old man with the letter lasted five weeks.) Sometimes it was simply the hopeless. But even as they were fading out of life, we were already eyeing their bundles and bracing ourselves to be the first at their side to strip them of that thicker pair of trousers, that warmer jacket. 'After the head is off, no one weeps over the hair,' we muttered to ourselves. 'The skinned lamb can't grieve that his wool's gone.'

But still I chose not to remember their faces. For the further we travelled, the further I was travelling from myself, learning to snatch a bread ration from a dying man, and water from the sick. Oh, it was a fine education – not least in how a man can be forever shivering with damp and cold, his belly empty, and still want to live.

And learn. I learned to sleep through curses and cries and endless futile noisy arguments. I learned not to wake through kicks and punches delivered blindly in the dark. I learned to eat mouldy black-boiled wheat with gusto while all around me swilled the slime from men too weak to wait for the daily walk at rifle point across deserted tracks to empty their bowels and bladders.

Even that daily task could teach me more than I thought.

'See that?' said Liv Ullavitch, a man in the next pen along, nodding one morning at the huge letters painted along the side of our truck: WE HAIL OUR GLORIOUS REVOLUTION.

I shrugged. I'd seen the slogan painted on so many

walls over the years, I'd barely given the words a glance.

'Look closer.'

'What's to see?'

He grinned at me. 'Yuri, are you blind? You climb in and out of this truck every day and haven't noticed?'

Already the guard was harrying us. But next day, when we stopped, I chose a place to unbutton where I could stare back at the truck. Liv was right. When you looked carefully, you could see something different about the last five letters. The paint looked fresher and, rather as if the signwriter had suddenly handed the task to an apprentice, the little crosslines finishing off the strokes were missing.

WE HAIL OUR GLORIOUS REVOLUTION.

And then I realized what Liv had seen from the start – that someone must once have painted over four letters and altered the last of the rest. Now I was grinning too. How long had this truck rolled over our huge great country bearing its counter-revolutionary message?

WE HAIL OUR GLORIOUS REVOLT.

Now, each time I clambered in and out, I had a purpose. Like an obsessed detective I peered and peered, stumbling against a different panel of the truck each day to rub my sleeve against a patch of mud here, a smear of grease there, until at last my labours were rewarded.

There, on the filthy underbelly of the truck, out of sight of the signwriter sent to repair the damage: a tiny splash of paint.

Yellow, again.

Oh, yes. An education.

Mostly I sat beside a man called Stanislas. He was a geologist who claimed he'd earned a twenty-year sentence for deliberately concealing reserves of tin ore underground.

'How did you hide them?' I'd asked without thinking, the first time we spoke.

'Hide them?' He'd laughed in my face. 'Young Yuri, have you not yet learned enough about your Motherland to translate a criminal sentence into plain words?'

My senses came back to me. 'I know! It was your job to dig for mineral ore, but you failed to find a seam.'

'Bright lad!'

'What I don't understand,' I remember asking him a couple of weeks into our journey, 'is how it all went so wrong.'

'All what?'

'What my mother believed in. You know. What everyone was marching for in all those parades.'

'You mean the "Glorious Future"?'

'That's right.'

Bursting with laughter, he waved an arm around the metal pen in which we sat. 'You might as well give it its real name now, Yuri. Call it the "Glorious Lie".'

A memory came back to me of Grandmother, all those years ago, saying the very same thing. But I persisted. 'When did things change, though? When did it all go wrong?'

Stanislas called to a man slumped against the wire partition dividing our section of the carriage from the next. 'Hey, Taditz. You were in the thick of it. Over to you!'

It took Taditz a while to respond, as if the history of the business now lay in such a broken past, it wasn't worth the effort of explaining. But in the end I pestered him enough to make him lift his head.

'At the start we were just trying to make it work. Better and faster.'

'The Revolution?'

'Yes. We didn't feel we had for ever, so we pushed things along.' His voice picked up. 'The people were in a parlous state, you see. There was no justice anywhere. When things are rolling along nicely, you can afford to take your time to primp things till they're right. But when you're trying to turn a pigsty into the most perfect and fair society there's ever been ...'

He sighed. 'Well, you can't run a revolution like a game of croquet – all "After you, please" and good manners. We thought what we were doing was so important, it didn't really matter which way we went about it. Ends justified means.' He leaned towards me and grasped the wire. It was as if he was a vibrant young man again. 'We all *believed*, you see. Back at the start, you would have had to be a *stone* not to have worked for change!'

'My mother was a believer,' I told him.

He looked at me as if I were a half-wit. 'Back then, anyone with either a heart or a brain was a believer.'

I asked my question again. 'So what went *wrong*?'

He shrugged. 'At first, not much. A few corners cut too sharp. Then, as the people who were suffering from that squawked out too loud, the arguments began. Some wanted to move faster, some to slow down or do it differently.'

'Is that when the Leaders began to fall out?'

'That was the start of it. And when you win a battle, the safest thing to do is call your opponent a traitor and get his portrait down from the wall. It keeps things tidy.' Across his face spread the ghost of a smile. 'The problem is, of course, that everyone has to keep up. You mustn't make the mistake of taking a week's break in the country. By the time you come back to town, you'll find you've inadvertently laid a wreath on the grave of someone who hasn't been a hero for five whole days. So you must be a traitor yourself!'

He grinned and waved a hand towards the other end of the pen. 'Ask Rubachenko.'

Someone leaned over to shake a sleeping body on the other side of the bunk as Taditz called, 'Wake up, Rubachenko! Tell the boy what you told us in the cell. How, in your library, it wasn't just the portraits that vanished, it was the books as well.'

'Tell him yourself,' growled Rubachenko.

Taditz cheerfully gave him the finger and turned back to me. 'Well, first his shelves thinned out. And then, it seems, new books began arriving with – fancy! – whole different stories inside them. Fresh heroes. Different beginnings. He claims there were even photographs that looked exactly like the old ones except for strange little spaces where some of the faces had vanished.'

'Did he speak up?'

'Did he, hell! He's not that stupid! No. All

Rubachenko did was make the mistake of cracking a little joke.'

'A joke?'

Taditz was chuckling. 'Oh, yes. It seems his secretary was a loyal creature who'd marched in so many parades that it had turned her brain. She wanted Rubachenko to join her in sending birthday greetings to Our Great Leader, and Rubachenko said, "Save your stamp money. Our Great Captain's far too busy rewriting the newspapers back to his birth to read any messages from us." '

When all the laughter quietened, I asked Taditz, 'So did she tell?'

'Shopped him that very same hour. Wouldn't you? After all, "failure to denounce" is treason. And no doubt like the rest of us, that poor woman has a family.'

'Still – telling on someone who simply made a joke? Just to stay safe.'

'Better than telling on him because you're still a True Believer.'

I couldn't see it myself. But all the other men who joined in the argument took Taditz's side. 'That's right. Saving your own skin is at least understandable. It's all those fools who blind themselves to what's going on who are the worst.'

'They simply help Our Great Leader heap heavier chains round our necks.'

On the discussion rumbled. I found myself thinking about the last time our train had stopped in a station. In came the guards as usual, with rifles at the ready to remind us that our carriage was labelled GOODS IN TRANSIT and goods don't speak. But by leaning my head against the window, I'd managed to peer between the slats to see the people trailing along the platform.

Luckier than us.

For them to know it, they would have had to see into our stinking box. But, not knowing we were there, no doubt they were wallowing in their own miseries. Their working days of ten or twelve hours or more. The long, long lines to get their pitiful food. Having to share their tiny apartments with two or more other families they hadn't chosen and didn't like. All of it showed in their drawn faces and their sour looks, their sheer hostility to one another, their irritation with their children.

And the same ghastly grey despair hung over the refugees we saw along the embankments or waiting to cross the track at the forest halts. The ones with handcarts might still have one or two pots or toys – even a bundle of clothing to see them through mid winter. Those without carts were stooped under their bundles, and it was easy enough to guess how far they'd come from how little they still carried.

So many people on the move! Some glanced at the train as it rattled past. Most kept their eyes on the path. Sometimes their sheer indifference would lead us to believe we were invisible – shut in some sort of ghostly vehicle – no longer part of the real world. I'd peer through the slats, keeping my fingers spread for fear of splinters ramming into my eye. The wide flat steppes had given way to wastes of white. The snow fell faster. The silence around us thickened. Though none of us spoke of it, we all knew that, by now, without the clothes we'd stripped from our dead companions, we would have been dead from the cold.

Over and over there would be mysterious halts – often at night. We'd hear the door scrape open. Torches would shine into the carriage. In came the guards, complaining about the stink. Then:

'Hands out for bread!'

'Can't find your bowl? Bad luck on you. Your share goes on the floor.'

Hours would pass. Then, just as mysteriously, there would be another jolt and we'd be off again.

Eleven weeks.

I had lost count, but Liv Ullavitch had paid attention to our daily progress, scratching on the side of the carriage a map of where he thought we were, and gouging out a line for each of the days.

One night I woke to the rattle of points, and shouts outside. I heard a scrambling in the next pen along the carriage and Liv's hoarse whisper. 'Give me some room. Let me stand. I want to look out.'

The men he'd disturbed were scathing. 'Why? So you can mislead us again? Confuse two station signs, and keep us waiting for some place that never comes?'

'Scoff at your own stupidity,' I heard Liv hissing back. 'You know as well as I that, even a week ago, without a town to shelter you, you would have burrowed through your hole only to freeze to death.'

Your hole, he said.

Burrow through your hole.

Throwing an arm across my eyes, I grunted as though as deep in sleep as those jammed in beside me. Carefully I used what little force of muscle I had left to shift the nearest away enough to turn my body over. Only a couple of men in the next pen along were still awake, their heads raised, glowering at Liv. Could it be true that all this time they had been using some sort of tool to cut a way out through the carriage floor?

If so, Liv's poor advice had made a mockery of the task. But he was right now. No one would stand a chance in these vast wastes of snow and this great cold.

Still, I was curious. All the next day I kept my eyes that way. With so many bodies sprawled about, it was impossible to tell what men in other pens were doing so long as their backs were turned. But finally we were all herded out, as usual, to stand at the track-side and fumble at trouser flaps and buttons with fingers too frozen to obey. And, on the way back up the ramp into the carriage, I made a pretence of stumbling.

It was an easy enough matter to fall, for just a moment or two, into the wrong pen. Sure enough, there, a few feet beyond the place where Liv stood to scrape his map and tick off days, was a spreading of straw. It was filthy and wet. Why hadn't it been kicked aside? What was it hiding? Could what Liv said be right? Had they been busy all the journey?

Well, what a waste! Because the very next day we were spilled out of that train into another. This one had stoves in each box car. Ah, so they did intend to keep us alive!

And this one took us on – through walls of woolly fog and under frozen stars, past steel-blue ramparts of solid snow – north, north and further north, till we were out of any landscape we might recognize, into a foreign world.

CHAPTER FOURTEEN

And so I finally came to see for myself those same 'white nights' of which my grandmother spoke: that strange white flush that blurs the landscape and bleeds it of all life. Even the edges of the hills around seemed to be shivering as though reflected in water. And time seemed suspended, as if the whole world – forests, boulders, dark river creeks and trees – were simply waiting.

But for what? Simply to watch us each morning as we shuffled in our dark drab lines out of the barracks? I'd stumble on, chivvied by guards with dogs, nursing first the raw sore on this foot, then the infected toes on the other. One whole long winter that had been the death of most of my companions on the train had taken its toll on me. I'd watched the others sicken and fall one by one, and by the time the last snows softened into the late spring thaw, I threw their bodies onto the cart without a thought, except for my grandmother's old saying: 'If you live in a graveyard, there isn't time to weep for everyone.'

Besides, I was haunted by the sense that my life too was over: there was nothing ahead and the only things left to me lay in old memories.

If I stayed alive at all. Because, up where we were, men passed through the camp like shoals of fish – off the trains, into the mines, and under the earth within weeks. 'The mincing machine', we called it, and watched how well it worked, even in our small camp. I used to wonder how many trainloads of men and women there must be endlessly rolling north, that they could wash in tides through such an outpost – only one of thousands. Word had it that things in other places were even worse, with guards shooting prisoners like birds for sport, and ordering others to take off their boots and coats so they could take bets on how long it would be before each froze to death at his work.

It took men differently. Fear clung around some like mist. From others, it fell as easily as a cloak dropped to the ground. In me, it sparked a streak of devil-may-care to add to the cunning that had been growing inside me since I first stumbled out of that lowered bucket and ran from the building site in fear of my life. That very first day we'd stumbled off the last train and onto the open trucks that carried us to the camp, I'd elbowed my way into the middle of the crush of bodies, away from the stinging crystals swept by the icy winds. When we arrived in the stockade, my only concern was to study the huts around us, and work my way back along the line of shuffling men till I was sure I'd find myself pushed into the sturdiest and best protected. And when, a day or so later, I was herded towards a lorry headed for the mines, I dared shout at a guard not all that much older than myself, 'But this is stupid! I'm a woodcutter. I'd be of far more use in the forest.'

He looked me up and down. 'You?'

'Yes,' I said bravely. 'I've been felling trees since I was two years old.'

He burst out laughing and turned to one of the older guards beside him. 'I hear you like a good bet. I'll wager you this boy can't fell a full-grown pine within an hour.'

The other looked so bored he might have bet his grandmother would float down on a gold cloud if it would have passed the time. 'Done!'

So, thanks to Igor's fine training, I became a wood-cutter. Next day I learned that the man who'd taken the bet and saved me from the mines was called Sly Joe, and much disliked. But from the moment I earned him that fistful of money, he went easy on me. The work was brutally hard, though. My palms soon hardened to two wide callouses. My soul began to shrivel. And always, always in the back of my mind was the thought that, when my ten years were over, my grandmother would be dead and, if they were still alive, my parents most likely lost without trace.

The months crawled by. Sometimes we worked in gangs, sometimes alone or in pairs. A frequent work-mate was a man called Arkady. Behind his back we called him the Holy Fool, and often, back in the hut at night, the others tried to torment him.

'A hard day, Arkady? What thoughts ran through your mind as the sleet sloshed in your boots and that sore spread on your hands? Did you think back on your stupidity, trading a wife, a home and a son for a belief held by only a few old biddies with so many worms in their brains they'll never think clearly again!'

He'd shrug. 'Amuse yourselves as you choose. I'll not deny the living God – for them or you.'

'But, Arkady! A lifetime of snow and ice and black flies so you can say the two words "I believe"? Even your precious God can't think that that's a bargain!'

'You live your own life. I'll live mine.'

'Trusting in a better to come! At least we've wits enough to know this is the only one we'll ever get!'

Arkady lowered his head. I guessed he'd fallen into quiet prayer in search of strength. The pack pursued him through his murmurings. 'Hush all your pointless babbling!'

'Time to grow up and stop believing in fairy tales.'

'Join us here, in the real world!'

There was a shout from one of the upper bunks. 'Leave the man be.'

Instantly someone else snarled, 'He's lucky it's only insults that fall on his head. I look his way each night, and I could cheerfully kick him into the next blizzard. How dare he sit there wrapped in his magic cloak of mumbo-jumbo? A man who could have chosen another life! Wasting away here! He is an insult to the rest of us who had no choice!'

The wave of fury took its time to settle. Arkady kept his head down, still mouthing his prayers. I asked myself how anyone could truly think there might be a caring God. Was Grandmother herself still mumbling prayers on my behalf? Even as the months crawled by and one more vicious winter came and went, was she still begging all the saints to keep me safe? No doubt some prisoners managed to bribe a guard to smuggle out their letters, but I had no means with which to haggle. In spite of that, did everyone at home still hope that I'd come back some day?

One morning in summer we were called from our woodcutting because of an accident at the mine. It took an hour or so to load the body carts. On the way back I took a chance on the man beside me – a newcomer off the last train – and steered the cart off the track towards a deep split in the earth that I had noticed after the spring melt.

'What's this?' the newcomer asked. 'Your own private burial ground?'

'As good a grave as any,' I muttered as he watched me drag the first broken body through the fringe of willow herb that hid the crevasse. I tipped the dead man over. 'Lose a few here on every trip and we've a better chance of staying out of it ourselves.'

He helped me at my black work, and as we spread the remaining bodies more evenly over the cart, he told me bitterly, 'I was a vegetable grower on my old communal farm. And if I'd dared lose as many turnips in one year as they've lost men this one day, they would have thrown me into jail.'

'Wait until winter,' I told him. 'Down at the real burial ground the frozen bodies end up stacked like logs.'

The newcomer made a wry face. 'I suppose you can't dump them here when the hole's packed to the brim with ice?'

'That's right.'

He sighed. 'And so their heap just grows higher.'

I couldn't help but grin. 'Not that much higher. We lay the ones on the top out carefully. Then, each time there's a fresh snow fall, we prise a few bodies off and hide them in the soft drifts.'

He beat at the cloud of mosquitoes eating away at his face. 'Why bother? The moment the thaw comes they'll be seen again.'

I burst out laughing. 'What sort of fool are *you*? As soon as the river's crust has thawed enough, we boot them in and send them tumbling out of sight to save ourselves the work of digging the burial pits even deeper.'

We hauled in silence till we reached the others. And, hours later, when we'd been ordered back to the clearing to make up the real day's work through the white night, he was still shaking his head.

'Five carts of dead men. All in one morning! Why, Death himself would doff his cap to them.'

The man beside us told him sourly, 'Don't you believe it. In one of my transit camps there was dysentery. And, after that, typhus so bad whole compounds emptied of men faster than they could bring in more to bury the dead, then catch it and die in their turn.'

I made the usual joke. 'Fine, Dov. You take the prize! You've seen the worst.'

'We gambled poorly,' he admitted. 'To get the extra rations, we kept the bodies back until they stank.'

Suddenly he stopped. No more than a pace from the path, a man was hanging from a rope coiled round a branch. His neck was awry. I realized with a shock it was the fellow we'd all seen only that morning, bent over a broken handsaw, moaning quietly, with tears running down his beard.

Dov stepped up closer. 'Poor sod!'

I thought he was about to cut the dead man down. But no. Those huge hands, stained for life from working with leather, began at once to peel the footcloths off the hanging body.

The newcomer spat. 'Death here, there, everywhere! What are the three of us now, except bags of live bones waiting to line the roads to' – he turned his burning eyes my way – 'the Glorious Future!'

And, after that, indifference took him. Each time guards threatened, he'd simply murmur, 'Hurry up and shoot. What do I care?' Like many round me, it only took him a few days to come to believe that we were all corpses in the making. What was the point in worrying any more when it would happen?

And I'm not stupid. I knew it was sheer luck, and luck alone, that Sly Joe's passion for gambling had saved me from an early death in one of the mines. I knew that every one of the days spent felling trees for pit props and dragging them back to the clearing was one more lucky one.

And luck runs out. I should have felt the same despair. Indeed, I tried. I'd shivered in the same bunks, tended the same raw sores, felt the same hunger. And yet . . .

Sometimes the sunlight had sparkled so brightly across the boundless sheets of snow. Or, in the stinging wind under the china-blue sky, I'd smelled the blessed spring melt. Once I'd stood under a tree and my heart sang to see the way its tall brave trunk soared up towards the clouds. I'd watched the eagles sailing overhead. I couldn't help it. Even something as simple as seeing the grayling twisting in the river could stir something hopeful in me.

And there were always, *always*, things to learn. About the guards – which ones had tempers, which had been seen to laugh, which ones paid no attention when they caught you cramming the bursting berries into your mouth in the short summers. I don't believe I ever came to hate them – after all, their lives were just as limited as ours, their days as long and empty, even if their only job was to watch us while we did the work.

We dragged a tree trunk past Sly Joe one morning as he sprawled on a grassy hummock, counting the winnings from his last bet. 'That's right,' Gregory muttered in between his desperate fits of coughing. 'We'll lift the rock. You do the groaning.'

'Why's he called Sly?' I asked when we'd been safely swallowed up again between the bushes.

'That one? Because his brain's the devil's workshop! He takes against a prisoner and, lo and behold, they're on the next truck to the mines. He owes a fellow guard a gambling debt and – would you believe it? – just as the money should be changing hands, the other's body is found at the bottom of the ravine. An accident?' He shrugged. 'Perhaps. The *first* time . . .'

'Why should his fellow guards risk playing cards with such a poor loser?'

'They don't – once they've been warned. And the replacements are mostly so young and green he wins their money off them fair and square. But even the squirrels in the trees know that the man's a villain, so the name sticks.'

I looked back between the trees to where Sly Joe had turned his boot caps up to the filtering sun. 'Is he asleep?'

'Yuri,' Gregory warned me. 'Never trust a guard's closed eyes. With lives so dull, they're looking for excuses to play with their guns.'

A timely reminder. I turned back to my work, and my luck held. Two years and more crawled past. Over a thousand days of hearing the thud of my axe and little else all through the day and through my dreams at night. The death of others was never far away. The rotten food claimed so many through the short burst of summer that I'd have been glad to see clouds gathering if I'd not known from hard experience that, within a week or two, the breezes would stiffen. Soon I would find my voice lifted away by chilly gusts, and realize I'd wished the horrors of that burning, biting season away too soon.

Autumn would come. Each time I was alone for even a moment in the clearing, I'd cram as many berries into my mouth as I could, knowing that soon I'd feel the stinging spittle of sleet and, only a day or so later, see the first sift of snowflakes. Within a week these berries would be hidden under unbroken humps of snow. The flanks of the hills would merge into a hard white veil that hung all around us, hemming us in place. And we'd be staggering once again through the dark days in the bone-chilling cold, our eyelids crusted with rime.

Another winter to dread, already on its way.

One night, after over half the men in our hut had failed to return, we inched our way closer to their bundles and waited, sunk in the deepest shame at what we were hoping to hear.

Word came soon enough.

'Another pit fall. They're all dead.'

Like the good scavengers we had become, we fell to fighting over the last few pitiful goods of other men's lives. Here was a pillow stuffed with something softer than wood shavings. There was a woollen face mask. Didn't Vasily have spare footcloths? And where was the wooden bowl of that Ukrainian who never spoke? It looked no larger than the others, but held a whole spoonful more.

Suddenly Dov lifted his shaven and disfigured head from his rooting to ask, 'How do they do it?'

I broke off from spreading my fingers around inside Ira's mattress, looking for hidden crusts.

'Do what?'

Dov waved an arm as if to pick out all the spaces

on the bunks now filled with ghosts of the dead. 'How can they suck the lives from so many men and not change their ways?'

Someone behind me muttered, 'The world is full of ravens. It always has been.'

'No,' Dov insisted. 'Even the famous killers in the past counted their victims only in dozens. And, leaving wars aside, I'll bet you could only lay the deaths of a few thousands at the door of the worst Czar.'

Between one fit of coughing and the next, Gregory asked irritably, 'So what's bothering you?'

Dov himself looked confused. But, keeping his hands on the two small bundles he'd fought for and won, he tried to explain things again. 'I'm saying that even a *rumour* of the sorts of numbers we know are passing through this camp would have made all the evil-doers of the past stop and take breath.'

I waited, but no one spoke.

'So what has changed,' said Dov, 'that Our Great Leader and his henchmen can have even an inkling of what they've set in train, and still keep on their bloody path?'

Most of the men still ignored him. But suddenly Jan Gobrek spoke up from his place in the corner. 'I understand your question. What does it take to kill in such numbers without human pity? Is that what you're asking?'

'Yes.' Dov's face cleared. 'That's what I want to know.'

'The answer's simple. All it takes is faith.'

'Faith?'

'Nothing more.' Jan gave the grin that showed the thorough way in which a guard had kicked his mouth to pulp for slowing a march. 'Faith has a dozen names. When I was in the university we called it *ideology*. In party lectures it's called *social theory*. If you burn people at the stake, you tend to call it *belief*. But, whatever its name, that's the ingredient missing in those who only go halfway.' He made a grimace of contempt. 'This pack of murderers has it in plenty.'

Dov's mouth had fallen open. '*Faith?* Are you *serious?*'

'It's all you need,' Jan told him firmly. 'A theory behind you, giving wind to your sails. What else would give them the determination to wade on through torrents of blood? What else could stop them hearing the cries of the orphans they've created, and the curses of their victims – even the reproaches of those they respect? It's faith. They're blinded by it. Fortified by it. So fortified that what they do seems good and worthy even if, done for any other purpose, those very same things would seem shocking, even to them.'

The silence that fell was broken by the usual warning ring of a hammer against a metal post. We gathered for the count. That night I had a whole bunk to myself for the first time, and wasted the hours fighting the fleas that wouldn't settle till the hammer swung again.

Another day. As we were shuffling towards the gates, two open trucks stuffed tight with men rattled to a halt outside.

I heard a voice behind me. 'They've wasted no time in filling dead men's boots!'

But we were so far from any transit camp that the new prisoners on the trucks must have been well on their way to us before the pit roof fell. We waited to see if we'd be marched out first, or if the guards would get the dogs to force us back, to march the newcomers in.

A chill and clinging mist hung over us. I stood and shivered. Which would it be? Us out? Them in? They'd spent the whole night in an open truck and it was obvious that more than a few were only held on their feet by the press of bodies around them.

But we were off to work.

And so, of course, we had our orders first. 'In your lines! Hands clasped behind you. March!'

We'd learned from the bitter experience of others never to call attention to ourselves by standing out from the crowd. Safer by far always to plod along as close as you could to the centre of any group, with eyes downcast. Still, it was easy enough to steal a glance as we trudged past. One of the men on the first truck was wrinkling his nose at the stink, and staring in astonishment at the vast hummocks of excrement behind the latrines.

Something about the way he stood, the way he moved, gave me a jolt.

Could it be? Could it?

Nikolai! The young daredevil who'd teased Sergei so well at Pioneer camp? Here? In our camp? My heart leaped. At last! A real friend. Someone my own age!

'Heads down! March faster!'

I bowed my head and splashed through the sea of mud around the stockade. To those stumbling along at my side, I must have looked as dismal as before. Inside I was singing. Already the daydreams had begun. Nikolai would escape the roll call for the mines. Like me, he'd end up on the forest detail. We'd work together day by day. We'd share our stories, and he would tell me how he'd guessed, even all that long time ago, that I was 'one of them' at heart. Yellow and black.

My excitement grew. This time, I knew, things would work out more evenly between us. After all, I'd be the one who knew more. I'd teach him all the tricks. In summer I'd be the one to show him how to protect himself against the burning sun and the vicious mosquitoes. In winter I'd warn him not to panic the first time he woke and found himself unable to lift his head. 'You won't be paralysed. It'll just be your hair frozen fast to the bedding.'

Perhaps he'd laugh, not quite believing me. I'd show him how to sleep with feet jammed into a jacket sleeve for extra warmth, and how to thicken his overcoat with rags, and wrap his face with more rags against the stinging winds.

At work too. When we were in the forest I'd show him how to cheat. Why fell a whole new tree when, in some nearby clearing, you're bound to find one cut down some other winter by someone too weak to drag it back. 'Cut off its ends to make it look fresh. We call it "making a sandwich".'

In short, I'd teach him the only wisdom I'd picked up: 'Scrape through today in any way you can, and hope for better tomorrow.'

All day I dreamed as I worked. Slowly the pale sun lifted, then all too soon set again. On came the blinding arc lights, and hours crawled by. At last the work shift ended. Back we all trudged, a herd of coughing, spitting, cursing shadows – all except one of them counting the heartbeats to the end of the day.

All except me.

CHAPTER FIFT

There he was, in one of the lines of men waiting to take the place of others in the food hut. I watched him shuffling towards the door, clutching his bowl, and wondered what he'd think of our rotten bread and spoiled cod – if we were lucky. I tried to guess if he'd be one of those who bolted down his daily ration the moment it was given him, or if he was a hoarder.

I'd tried it both ways. If you gobbled, not just your gruel, but the bread too while you were in the food hut, then work next day was even more of a misery. But save your bread till morning and you lay awake all night – and not just from hunger. From under the bundle you used as a pillow it tempted you. *Eat me! I might get stolen. Anything might happen. It would be better to eat me now.* That tiny lump of bread called to you through dreams of food you hadn't seen since your arrest: tomatoes, apples, cucumber, butter ... *Don't wait another moment. Eat me now!*

So in the food hut I took my place on the bench with the rest of my work team. At the end of a day in the forest food came before anything, even renewing what I was already thinking of as an old friendship. To peel my attention away for a moment from the division of our group's ration was to risk losing my share.

And then I heard the voice I remembered so well, clear as a bell. 'How can you *speak* like that? Clearly some things have gone wrong, but only because of the devilish tricks of those who oppose Our Leader. They keep on trying to lead the Revolution off its path.'

The men around kept eating. You could see it on their faces: what does one fool matter in a country ruled by a madman?

But Thomas had, as usual, wiped his bowl so clean that he was licking at the shine. And no one left this warm hut till they were pushed out at rifle point. So out of mischief he asked my Nikolai, 'Why are you here, then? Surely a loyal young man like you should still be out there, working towards the Glorious Future.'

'It's a mistake,' said Nikolai. 'Some accident of paperwork. A misunderstanding. I've every faith it will be sorted out. I won't be here for long.' He shook his head. 'No, I'm quite sure it won't be more than a month or two before word comes to release me.'

Even the steady eaters were pricking up their ears now. All thought of foolishness was left aside. Here was a gift indeed! A newcomer ready to remind them of old times around a table. After all, many of the men clung to old pastimes. All around, when work ended, there were gamblers, smokers and cardsharps to be seen – even men singing melancholy songs on home-made balalaikas.

But no one had yet preserved enough of his old self to play the buffoon.

'So tell us, lad,' cried Dov, happy to take the bait now that all his food was safe inside his belly. 'What else will be sorted out in a month or two? The fact that the only crops this Great Leader of ours has ever managed to harvest is "enemies of the people"? The problem that not all villages have traitors, but since every village must be terrorized, every village must be found to contain some? The fact that . . .'

I was distracted from my pride in watching Nikolai's success in entertaining the men. His colour was rising. How fine an actor could he be? Surely not skilled enough to raise those spots of anger on his cheeks, and set that tiny nerve trembling across his cheekbone?

Now he was interrupting Dov. 'These are small matters! Mere misprints in the great unfolding of history!'

Something in the tone of his voice caused a sickening drop in my spirits. Surely no one – not even those who acted on the stage – could do so good a job of laying claim to false opinions. Could it be possible that Nikolai wasn't clowning to amuse us all, and what we heard was what he truly thought?

Could he *believe* this?

I thought back to what I'd heard him saying all those years ago about those men who fought without weapons or boots. Now, I knew well enough from talk around me that, far from being willing volunteers, those poor doomed souls had been from punishment battalions. It was at gunpoint that they'd been herded over the bloodsoaked earth towards the enemy tanks that rolled over their bodies. Could I have been mistaken, even back then, in thinking that Nikolai was taking a rise out of our old team leader? When he'd pushed back his helmet and stood with that seraphic smile, reminding me of the holy man in Grandmother's print, could he have been in as much ecstasy? Thrilled at the very idea of sacrifice? Ready and willing to be a new sort of martyr – not for a God but for a Cause?

So had I been mistaken all this time? Could he have been *sincere*?

Certainly Dov no longer thought this newcomer was playing games and being comical.

'Mere *misprints*?' He spread his hands. 'That's what you call the countless hundreds and thousands of men like us? *Misprints*?'

'The Leader knows what he's doing. The Leader knows that what he's aiming for is—'

Dov's hand slammed down. 'The Leader's a *fanatic*. A man who, even as he loses sight of where he's going, works even harder to get there.'

They were all at it now, scorching Nikolai with their fury. 'Killing more men!'

'Filling more camps and prisons.'

'The "Great Friend of Families" – conducting a war of blood against his own people!'

Dov thrust his face across the greasy boards. 'The man's an *oaf*. His thinking is so primitive that he's indifferent to losses.'

'Not true!' insisted Nikolai. 'He simply knows that it's important to crush the enemy within before he moves on.'

'The enemy within!' Dov turned to his neighbours

and scoffed. 'Here is a boy who'll no doubt happily freeze to death rather than put on a jacket in the colours yellow and black.'

Nikolai spat. 'Yellow and Black! Those traitors! But we will crush them. Crush them without mercy.'

Dov snarled, 'You'd follow him even in that? You'd manage to convince yourself, just as he has, that pitilessness is a *virtue*?'

Nikolai raised his voice so even the guards could hear. 'Why not? He is Our Leader! Wiser by far than us. How can we question him? No doubt, in an ideal world, he'd care for each and every one of us. But how is he to be blamed if, in the Great March towards the Common Good, a few people suffer?'

Dov spat. 'A charming fellow, no doubt – when he's asleep!'

A man I'd never before seen open his mouth leaned down the table. 'That's a part of the problem, of course. The bloody man never does sleep. Take it from me, I worked for those who worked for him. And even way back then this "Incomparable Strategist" of ours was sitting up all night signing orders for executions. Friends, colleagues, strangers – he didn't care! It could take hours and hours. Sometimes he sat for so long snuffing out other people's lives, they took to calling him "Stone Arse".'

I stared at Nikolai. He seemed to be shrinking back in terror at the thought of sharing a few greasy planks of wood with such a pack of traitors. And I kept staring. What I had seen on everyone's faces when he first spoke up was sheer indifference, or, if they'd safely emptied their bowls, a spark of interest – even, in the liveliest, a little amusement.

That had turned to doubt. Then incomprehension. After that came pity. But now they were once again looking at Nikolai with the most simple-hearted amusement. Even an hour later, back in the hut, I heard a chuckle beneath me. Peering over the edge of the bunk, I saw Gregory comforting himself as usual between his coughing fits by running the ends of his fingers around the swirling curlicues of faded pattern on the sleeves of his thick quilted jacket.

'Something amusing?'

'Misprints of history!' repeated Gregory, and chuckled himself into another vicious fit of coughing. The rest took up the theme. And for the rest of the evening odd echoes of what Nikolai had said floated around our hut – 'Mere misprints!' 'Wiser than us!' 'These are small matters' – setting off roars of laughter.

The friend I had imagined. Come, and gone, all in one day.

And after that, all I could think of was escape. Don't ask me why. Perhaps it was disappointment that the one person with whom I'd felt some kinship, on whom I'd pinned some hope, had proved to have even less substance than the stinging crystals of fog through which we tramped to work.

Everyone warned me. 'Forget it, Yuri. Escape's impossible.'

'If you stop eating to hoard the food you'll need, you'll be dead before you start.'

'Set off in winter and you'll freeze. In summer, you'll drown in the bogs.'

'Look around you, boy. Why do you think there are no fences around the places where we work? This is a natural prison.'

And they were right, of course. Impossible to go north. The east was barred by mountain ranges. To the south lay that enormous inland sea few crossed the other way – and only then with special papers. And no one could recall that sense of being carried over endless space and not face the fact that there were hundreds of miles to be retraced even to reach those last few squalid huts we'd seen on the last northward stretch of our great journey.

Still, others had tried it. I heard of a group of prisoners who'd lured a truck of soldiers off the road into a ravine. They'd all escaped in the ensuing chaos. And though most were rounded up and shot out of hand, some got away. Could one or two have made it out of this frozen waste to more hospitable country where they could hide in the woods and live off what they could find – what the older men called with a chuckle 'serving in General Cuckoo's army'?

Or had the fierce walls of white defeated them, leaving their bodies to rot in the next spring thaw?

I wasn't the only one to brood on thoughts of escape. The very next day I watched a man with a bad limp trade a whole lump of bread for some small scrap of metal Oleg had picked up at work.

The moment he'd hobbled off, I braved the cutting wind to cross the compound and ask Oleg, 'What did he want with that?'

Oleg just shrugged. So it was left to me to work my way close enough to the half-lame man in the next headcount to catch him whispering the word 'north' to his companion.

North? Why should a man say 'north' when the only words needed were 'shovel' and 'bread', 'work' and 'cold'? Was it a compass he was hoping to make out of his twist of metal?

And why not? Even the walking skeleton they called Old Georg had spent whole hours gleaned from stolen minutes polishing two lengths of wood. Now they were hidden in some hollow tree along with his fantasy: 'They'll make good skis. They'll see me through the valley.' Surely not all the dreams we clung to were as hopeless as his. Tales filtered in from other camps. The prisoners in one work party had scattered in a blizzard. The men in another had jumped their guards and shot them with their own guns.

'It can be done, then!'

The men around me laughed. 'Oh, yes! Once you're away from the camp, the rest is easy!'

'Angels swoop down to lift you on their wings and carry you over a thousand miles of snow and ice.'

'And drop you safely in the city.'

'Along with a picnic basket to keep you going till you find a job where no one asks to see your papers.'

Again they all hooted with merriment. 'Yuri, face it! You'll still be here with us as long as you have a hole in your arse!'

But hope is not some dried leaf you can let fall and watch blow away in the wind. I spent my days imagining each step of my escape. The strange hut barnacled with ice I'd happen across by sheer good luck as I stumbled through the forest. The kindly old man who'd share his last loaf with me just as my strength failed. The cart that would rumble by, with an axle just deep enough to hide on.

And last – most blessed of all – the snaking steam train that would slow for the rise just as the guard was looking the other way . . .

I'd look up, only to realize that what had startled me was my own voice. I had been singing. Singing! So near did freedom seem!

But it was only a daydream: a thin safe braid of imaginings through which I could weave my own path, choose my own ending. The dreams I had at night followed a different pattern. Then, I would find myself beside a door I'd never seen before, set in the stockade. It had no lock and I knew on the other side there would be sunshine, apples! My mother would be there, her arms outstretched. Weeping with happiness, I'd tumble through – only to hear mocking laughter and find myself falling into black, black night.

No. Better to stick to daytime fancies as we worked, and marched, and stood in endless lines.

'Stay back there! Second count!'

'What is the *point*?' Tarquin grumbled. 'They barely care who we are. Why should they care how many of us they let in or out?'

And why indeed? From time to time the guards would take against a prisoner. (It seemed to me they took an especial pleasure in ordering poor Nikolai onto the next truck to the mines.) But on the whole they went through their miserable routines as sourly as those they herded to and fro.

We stamped our feet, and bound our face-cloths tighter against the bitter sleet. At last the doors in the stockade opened like jaws to draw us all back in. We stumbled to the shelter of the hut, with Tarquin still complaining.

Sensing some entertainment, one of the men began to tease. 'Would you prefer them to make more sense of the counts by giving us back our papers to be inspected time and again?'

Tarquin snorted. 'A fine show that would be! Half the dolts can't read. They'd just stare at the page, then either take against your face and kick you senseless, or let you go.'

From Gregory's bunk beneath came one of those great storms of coughing we knew would soon be the death of him. I heard the weak rasp of his voice: 'What difference would that make? Our papers are a sham. I begged the stubborn oaf who gave me mine, "Do I *look* eight years old? Somebody's going to arrest me for travelling on false papers because you've written one number so carelessly it looks like another." But would he lift his pen to change it? No. And now I'm going to cough the last of my guts up in this filthy hut.'

A commonplace enough story. It had no power to shock. So I can only think that it was pity for a man so close to death that made me lean over the side of the bunk to say, 'That's why you're here? A simple mistake in your papers?'

Gregory tried to hide whatever ghastly stuff it was he was spitting into his food bowl. And when he spoke again, it was as if he were offering comfort to me, not the other way round.

'Yuri, you know as well as I do that the very next morning I would have made the mistake of looking too long at some important bridge. Or said "Good morning" to someone a neighbour had just been kicked into denouncing.'

Another fit of coughing choked him before he could finish up weakly, 'What does it matter?'

But still, it ate at me. Such a sweet man, and so close to his grave. At least I'd brought disaster on myself with my own tongue. Through autumn winds so strong that you could lean on them, through all the blinding whorls of winter storms, I burned with frustration. These were my best years that were trickling away. The seasons when I should have lived, and loved, and felt my strongest, were one long suffering grind.

And those around me must have seen my restlessness and desperation. For one day, in the column for the count, someone called Vasim touched his arm to mine and whispered, 'See who is watching you.'

I glanced the way Vasim twisted his rag-covered hand. Sure enough, in the next column, that towering man we were all in the habit of calling the Bear had turned his head into the bitter wind to look my way.

The call rang out. 'Heads down! Your hands behind you! March!'

And we were off again. But that night was the same. As we stood stamping on the filthy snow, impatiently waiting our turn to get back through the gates and into the shelter of the huts, the Bear's eyes were on me.

No one around me knew any more about him than I could see with my eyes. 'The Bear? I'll tell you this much. He has bigger thumbs than brains!'

'Born with steel mittens, that one.'

'The Sublime Strategist certainly missed a trick not offering a man like that a job in his prison cellars. He could tear the wings off an eagle.'

Still he looked my way. Gradually I came to notice he wasn't the only one taking an interest. Time and again through the long second count, a man with a wild frizzy beard also kept turning to look me up and down.

'He's called Leon,' Dov whispered, adding admiringly, 'A smart one, that. He certainly knows how many beans in a bag make five.'

I heard my grandmother's voice, 'Curly hair, curly thoughts!' and took to wondering for the millionth time if any of my family were still alive, and if so, how they managed. The man called Leon failed to look my way again – not that day, or the next – and so I gave him little thought until a few mornings later, when he was ordered from his place at the front of his column to clear a drift of snow that had banked up against the stockade, hemming us in.

When the great gates were finally hauled open, he failed to move away. Making great play of ramming the shaft of his shovel deeper down into the blade, he managed to linger long enough to bark out a word like a cough as I went past.

'La-*trine*!'

I heard it clearly. *Latrine*.

I knew the message was for me. I had no doubt. And I was sure he meant that very night. All day I put the meeting out of my mind. Who was to say this wouldn't be the morning some guard lost patience and shot him? Or perhaps he'd be standing in view when someone realized they were a few men short for the next convoy to the mines. 'Here! You! You! And *you*!'

Three more lives over. And no one for me to meet over those heaps of shit once more too frozen to be moved till spring.

But he was there. When our hut was herded out, he was the only one of his group still to be squatting, feigning a running sickness.

I took a place beside him on the planks.

At once he spoke. 'I hear your mind is on escape.'

'Not mine,' I told him promptly. 'You must be mistaken.'

He'd have dismissed me for a fool if I'd said anything else. Brushing my caution aside, he told me, 'You stand no chance alone. So come with us.'

'Us?'

'Me and the Bear.'

We'd had no more than a moment and he was still pretending to be busy with his business. But already a guard on the watchtower was turning his rifle our way. Quickly Leon rose from his squat and, fumbling with his clumsy home-made buttons, set off for his own hut.

I watched him go – a strong-looking man with a firm stride. That night, between my thin shivering dreams, the thought came back over and over.

Who *better* to travel with than him and the Bear? And, by the morning, who *else*?

CHAPTER SIXTEEN

From that day on, I started to keep back scraps from
each day's ration: a lump of bread, a thread of gristle
as strung out as my own nerves. I smuggled them out
of the stockade hidden in the cloths round my face.
That way, if there was a search, I could at least get
their benefit. I'd plod along in utter misery, resisting
the temptation to see each guard's threatening glance
as the excuse to swallow the precious mouthfuls to
stave off my burning hunger. Once we reached the
clearing, I'd wait for a quiet moment to ram
the morsels, one by one, day by day, into the rag bag
of other frozen pieces I'd hidden deep in the snow
under a bush.

Now that our paths had crossed, I seemed to see
the man who'd approached me time and again – now
standing in line for a headcount, now with his arms
protectively round his bowl in the food hall. But,
from a host of casual questions to those around me,
I learned no more about Leon than that no one knew
any harm of him, and some admired his wits. Clearly

he had the skill of fending off attention – always a good thing in the camp. And, like me, he must have had good luck, or he'd already have been down the mines.

Twice, in the weeks we waited, I risked trying to cross his path in the compound. The moment he saw me, he'd move aside, or, if that was difficult, murmur no more than, 'Be patient!'

But as the black winter days crawled towards spring, I worried more and more. What did I know of whatever plan they were hatching? Not a thing. How was it possible to steel myself for an escape when I had no idea whether we'd all be breaking out together from inside the stockade, or if I'd be going on the run from my workplace, and joining the two of them later on the run from their own.

One morning I saw Leon and the Bear working together to repair one of the struts on a watchtower. The snow was falling thickly and, with their backs turned, I hoped to take them by surprise and demand some answers – perhaps even threaten to bail out unless they trusted me with at least the bare bones of the plan.

As I came close, the Bear looked up. I heard him murmuring, 'Here comes our little beam of hope.'

His sniggering tone annoyed me. I couldn't help

but show my irritation. 'You tell me nothing! What are you planning? And when?'

Without a word, the Bear walked off as if to fetch another length of wood from the nearby pile. 'Soon, soon,' Leon soothed me. 'You know as well as I do, the less we tell you, the safer you are. But everything's falling in place.' He grinned. 'And it will work. Believe me, we'll get clear away.'

'But how will we travel?' I persisted. 'And what about provisions? I can't get far on the few scraps I've managed to keep back. So tell me how—'

Already he was striding out of hearing. I thought of going after him, but came to my senses. Leon was right. The less I knew, the fewer ways I could let slip a secret and the less could be kicked out of me afterwards if I did. These two were careful men, and I should be grateful that, hearing how desperate I was, they had agreed to take me as a companion. I must watch my step in case they thought better of their decision, and left without me.

One night I found a scrap of paper tucked into the bundle on my bunk. 'Tomorrow.'

Tomorrow?

Instantly terror tore into me, disguised as reason. Forgetting the fact that, as the spring melt advanced, the guard on us tightened, I let the cowardly excuses for inaction breed in my brain. Why *now*, before the thaw had set in fully? At least if we waited till spring was further advanced we could perhaps help ourselves by lashing logs into a raft and, with the river flowing freely again, be far from the camp in hours.

But then, one small mistake and we'd be in the water, paralysed within moments from cold. Or, rounding a bend, we might find ourselves shot at from the watchtowers of other camps we hadn't known about that were along the way.

Just as I tried to fortify myself against one real fear by inventing others, Gregory coughed beneath me – weakly, almost apologetically.

By the time I noticed the silence, he was gone.

What shameful cunning desperation teaches us. Knowing how firmly I'd be pushed aside by tougher inmates, I clambered down and, shielding Gregory's body with my own, kept talking as if he could hear me – even interrupted myself with coughs as harsh as I could manage – while I tugged off his precious quilted jacket, stiff with dirt.

I didn't dare announce the death till I had safely wriggled into it.

'Gregory's gone.'

There was the usual rush to strip his body and

bundle of all things useful. Dressing him in our cast-off rags, we carried him over to the chilliest bunk, knowing that if we said nothing to the guard and milled about enough to cause confusion, we would at least get one extra ration to share between us before the next count.

But, coming back from the food hut, I couldn't help glancing, over and again, at that dark heap. Was this what death made of us? Suddenly all hope that my escape might follow the pattern of my idle day-dreams drained away. I saw that all that lay ahead was certain death. I knew at once I must seek out my co-conspirators in the dawn headcount and shake my head – make it quite clear to them that I'd with-drawn from their venture.

Better to suffer anything, year after year, than end up like Gregory – a stick of cold flesh wrapped in filthy rags.

I was determined. But even before the hammer had struck the fence post the next morning to summon us for the first count, Sly Joe stepped into our hut.

He looked around carefully, then picked me out. 'You, boy! A burial detail.'

I took it the guards had somehow picked up the fact that one of our men had died. Knowing Sly Joe was not a man to cross, I hastily pulled on the last of my face-wraps and moved towards the bunk on which Gregory's body lay.

Sly Joe stepped in front of me. 'Stop dallying! Obey the order! Get out there! Now!'

Baffled, I stumbled to the door. Winter, it seemed, had come back in force overnight to take one last fierce bow. Outside, the cold hit like a wall.

Sly Joe pushed me towards two shadows waiting beside the hut. My fellow conspirators! The Bear eyed me warily. Leon's face was blank. I wondered by what strange sort of cunning he'd managed to fix things so that a guard – even one as self-serving and dishonest as Sly Joe – would round us up together. None of the prisoners had any money. There were no women in our camp who might have been persuaded to barter favours. Clever as Leon might be, what could he possibly have found to offer to make Sly Joe willing to rise out of turn before the dawn, and escort the three of us over the compound together?

Falling in step, we followed each barked order. Against the guards' hut on the furthest side, two bodies lay slumped – both, from the look of them, the victims of a savage beating. Leon and I took hold of the first and staggered across the compound, out of step. The Bear threw the other across his shoulder and walked as easily as if the dead man weighed little more than a shawl.

Snow fell so fast, the bodies were blanketed even before we reached the stockade gates. After a shout from Sly Joe, a shovel landed at my feet.

I dropped my end of the body. The eyes flew open. 'Get those gates open! Hurry and dig!'

I went at it with a will, desperate to be done with the job and away from the empty stare of those dead eyes. Soon I had cleared enough for one of the gates to be opened a crack, to let our small work party out.

There, on the other side, the outside guard stood stamping his feet, waiting for the end of his shift. I didn't recognize his face, and knew he must be fresh to the camp. After a week or so, the only concern of most of the guards on overnight duty was to stay in the shelter of the watchtower.

Sly Joe called out to him, 'Two bodies for the stack.'

The new guard looked our way. Recognizing our escort, he shouted, 'Hey, Joe! A word with you, if you please!'

But with a snarl to the three of us – 'Keep walking!' – Sly Joe headed back to the gates.

The new guard shrugged. Calling us to order, he followed as we slipped and staggered down the track with our unwieldy burdens. Blinded by snow, we almost missed the narrow path down to where all the frozen corpses lay stacked, waiting for the thaw. By now, Leon and I no longer had the strength to carry our body and took to hauling it over the snow as if it were a sled.

Halfway down the steepest slope, it started sliding from its own sheer weight. I took the chance to ease my aching back and, as I drew myself up, I saw a shadow in the woods behind.

Someone was following.

Before I could murmur to Leon, the guard took a threatening step towards us. 'Stop your slacking!'

With him so close, his gun already in his hand, I left off all thoughts of whispering. In any case, the man behind us might be part of Leon's plan. What did I know? He'd kept the day of the breakout from me until the last minute. Wasn't it possible that there were four of us, not just three, in this escape?

With one last scramble down the snowy track, we reached the river's crust. To the side lay the great winter pile of bodies, square and still, peacefully shrouded in white.

Single-handed, the Bear heaved up the load he'd been carrying. As the body landed, the gathered snow flew off in giant puffs, to leave a streak of dark rags sprawled over humps of white.

Leon and I rolled our own burden up against the edge of the stack.

'On the top!' shouted the guard.

A tiny moment of spite. No one would come down here, except to dump more corpses. What did it matter how the pile was stacked?

But guards are guards. So, to protect ourselves from meeting the same brutal end as the man we'd been carrying, Leon and I began to swing his body to and fro, trying to muster the energy to hurl it upwards.

A sharp sound rang out from between the trees.

Curious, the guard moved round to the other side. Leon and I took the chance to ram the body back where we'd put it at the start. While Leon heaped fresh snow over to disguise it, I clambered up to brush snow off one of the bodies on the top.

'There!' Leon said, satisfied. 'Now let the bastard tell one corpse from another.'

The guard was still peering cautiously between the trees. I slid back down, using the frozen elbows and feet of dead men as footholds. The guard came back, still glancing over his shoulder, and signalled us to start the trek back to the camp.

I moved obediently onto the path, but Leon and the Bear stood firm, staring between the trees.

To my astonishment, out stepped Sly Joe, whom we'd last seen heading so determinedly back to the stockade gates. His gun was drawn. Before I even had time to wonder which of our lives he'd snuff out first merely for cheating a fellow guard on where we put the body in a heap, the shot rang out.

The sharp sound bounced off the river's crust and echoed around the forest.

So. Not me. I might be next, but curiosity can last as long as the heart beats. I heard the echo of my grandmother's voice – 'Must you be wise as a tree full of owls?' – as I opened my eyes to see which of the others lay sprawled in the snow.

It was the guard – spreadeagled backwards with a look of astonishment on his face and a neat red stain in the middle of his forehead.

The *guard*?

In utter bafflement, I turned. But Sly Joe was already vanishing between the trees.

And then at last it came to me. What better plan than one that did away with a man to whom he owed money? Three prisoners disappear, leaving a guard shot dead – no doubt with a bullet from his very own gun. No more thought needed!

I turned to Leon with a new respect. Even if he had known about a new gambling debt, how had he managed to broker such a deal between himself and Sly Joe? How did—?

'Yuri!' Already Leon and the Bear were stripping the guard of his uniform. There was a bit of cursing, a few grunts, and yet another corpse lay on the top of the pile.

The Bear pulled out the body Leon and I had wedged along the side. As if another man's soft shell were no more to him than an old tarpaulin, he tossed it upwards.

'Yuri! Get up there again. Lay this man over the guard to hide his body.'

Within the hour these bodies would be frozen in the stack like all the others. It would be that long – longer, if we were lucky – before the alarm was even raised.

A brilliant plan! I could have fallen at Leon's feet. And kissed the Bear's hands! His brute strength. His cool indifference. Masterly!

We turned our backs on the path back to the stockade. From the lie of the river, I knew that we were setting off towards the west.

It was still early morning. Snow was still falling as we strode away.

CHAPTER SEVENTEEN

What can I tell about my fellow travellers? Less than you'd think since, with our frostbitten faces bound with cloths from crown to chin, we kept our mouths shut as we struggled over the snowy wastes day and night like three shadows. Even when it was my turn to wear the guard's thick greatcoat, my lungs and ears were filled with the force of the cold. But we were on our way. And such is the difference between senseless suffering, and suffering to a purpose, that what would have been unbearable was almost gladly borne.

I learned the Bear's name was Oskar. I learned he'd been a railwayman. I learned he had a wife and son whom he'd not heard from in years, since his arrest. And, on the day I slid into the ravine, I learned how fast he could move. Before I'd even fallen past the first overhang, he'd shot out a hand and pulled me out with no effort.

'Up you get, Yuri. Don't want you dead yet.'

About Leon I learned nothing. While we were on

the move he rarely spoke, except to order me to pay attention to the track. And that made sense. With drifts so high, a man could tumble and suffocate before his friends could scramble halfway down to him. Before this last unexpected blizzard, the thaw had been well on its way. It was impossible to be certain what lay beneath the mounds of snow. Safer by far to stick to the roadway. And since at any moment you might raise your ice-encrusted eyes to see a truck approaching, silence was wise.

But there is silence and silence. When we were walking, there was at least the rhythmic creak of ice beneath our cloth-wrapped boots. When we drew to a halt, there was a silence so deep, so unnatural, you'd think that all the noise in the world had been swallowed for ever.

We stopped as little as we could. With cold that sent such tremors through the body, there was no comfort in rest. We only settled when we stumbled on places where we might keep a fire alight – in an abandoned guard post, or a natural ice hollow.

Leon would draw out the little wooden box he'd brought from the camp. Crouched with his back to the wind, he'd use the primitive flint lighter someone in camp had traded for a pair of boots. While he set fire to the pine needles and the little store of kindling we'd kept dry under our clothes, I'd scurry round to find more for the next day.

Then I'd delve in the cloth bag I'd dug out hurriedly the day we left, as we passed through the clearing. Already my supplies were so meagre that I was reduced to comforting myself by sucking grease from the cloth.

'Never mind.' Oskar winked at Leon as they divided up their own scraps. 'Soon we'll be eating like kings.'

'Hush, fool!' snapped Leon.

'Juicy steaks, dripping—'

'Quiet, I said!'

Had talk of food in plenty made Leon's stomach groan? 'We have the guard's gun,' I reminded him. 'Why not go hunting?'

Oskar gave me a grin. 'Why waste a bullet on some skinny winter bird when we can fell meat your size with a strong fist?'

Fell meat my size?

He meant a young reindeer, surely? Or a bear cub.

But still, unease took its grip. A dreadful thought flashed through my brain. Why had they chosen me to come along with them? They didn't need a third – and certainly not a boy neither strong nor experienced – not even a friend. I thought of the guard whose stupid innocence had led to his own death and our escape. Was it possible that, far from being one of the beneficiaries of Oskar's strength and Leon's cunning, I was about to become one of the victims?

I heard the echo of Grandmother's voice. 'Yuri, your head is full of spinning motors!'

For a moment I took it for comfort – as an assurance that what was running through my mind was pure imagination, nothing more than macabre fantasy.

But she had always said it, not as a warning but in simple admiration.

Why?

Because I was usually *right*.

Already Leon was trying to distract me. 'At last the fire's caught! And as the track we're following widens, we're bound to move faster.'

But I'd not missed the warning glance he'd shot at Oskar. The world seemed suddenly more dangerous. I felt as if I were above my own body, looking down. I rummaged for some idle thing to say and heard myself, almost like a stranger, asking a question to which I'd known the answer since my first winter in camp.

'Leon, do you remember that, back in the coldest

days, there was a rustling that hung around us. Do you know what it was?'

Before, when I'd asked a question, he'd simply scowled. This time, as if to prove that we were all good friends together around the camp fire, he took the trouble to answer.

'That? It's called the whispering of the stars.'

'The whispering of the *stars*?'

I made it sound as if I'd never heard the words before. I didn't turn from the fire, but still I saw the way Oskar was looking at Leon, as if to say: 'See? Put away your worries. Already the stupid boy's mind is off on other matters.'

I battened down nausea. But, with my mind still racing down other paths, it was important to keep up my idle questioning. 'What makes the rustling noise, though?'

'Your own breath as it falls.'

'Falls? How?'

Leon shifted with impatience. 'When it's so cold, breath freezes straight to grains of ice. That rustle comes as they fall around you.'

I raised my eyes, all innocence. 'That will be something to tell my family when I get back!' Then, knowing that in his urge to keep me calm lay my best chance to learn a thing or two about the journey they'd planned, I asked him, 'When will that be? We can't walk all the way. How will we travel?'

'Just as we came,' he told me. 'There's no other way.'

'By train?'

He turned to Oskar. 'Tell him.'

Oskar picked a stick out of the hissing fire and drew a cross in front of his huge ancient boots. 'Here is the camp.' He drew the stick across. 'And here's our path – westwards.' Lifting the stick a third time, he swept it down in a curve that cut across the path we'd be travelling. 'And here's a train line.'

Remembering the map so painstakingly scratched along the side of the truck on which I'd travelled all that time ago, I took a stick to draw a second line. 'But *this* is how we got here. The line runs much further south.'

'Who was it worked on the railways?' Leon asked sharply. 'You, or the Bear?'

Oskar cut his stick deeper into the runnel he'd drawn before. 'This line runs straight from the mines. It has no staging posts or holding camps. And since the trains carry ore and precious metals, the line's not on the maps.'

I made a face. 'It can't go very far west and stay a secret.'

'No need.' He pointed with the stick. 'The lines meet here. A short way north of Treltsky.'

It was important not to raise suspicion. I tossed my charred stick back in the fire. 'Walking's enough for me. I'll leave the planning to you two. If our escape from the camp is anything to go by, I'm in good hands.'

'Oh, yes,' said Oskar with a tiny smile. 'You're in good hands.'

I scrambled to my feet, clutching my belly. 'You'd think from how little we've eaten there'd be no reason for my bowels to slacken.'

They took no interest as I wandered off between the trees as if in search of some sheltered spot to attend to my business. I hoped the cold would dull their wits just enough for them not to count minutes. How far could I get? I might be young and starved and tired, but I had something inside me to give me strength.

Terror. The realization that a boy who's desperate can be plucked as easily as a peach. I pushed the branches aside and stood, ice crystals spinning and the ground as hard as iron under the rags on my feet. At last I was thinking it. At last the sense of it had wormed its way into my frozen brain. Hadn't I *listened*? I'd heard the Bear let out his little teases, and I'd thought nothing of them. 'Here comes our little beam of hope.' 'We don't want you dead yet.' 'Why waste a bullet on some skinny winter bird when we can fell meat your size with a strong fist?'

Could the threat have been any clearer? Had I been deaf as well as stupid?

I was their only way forward.

I was the meat.

Should I wait? Trust this was not the night the Bear would reach out to fell me? And would he even bother to be sure that I was dead before—?

No!

And if I couldn't let the thought so much as run through my brain, how could I risk it?

Should I hurry away in the darkness? But we had walked for days. I'd barely a scrap of food. Why should I stagger off alone to what would only be a slower death?

Snow crystals whirled around my head. Thoughts whirled inside it. The guard's coat was on my back now, but Leon would call for his turn to wear it at any moment. Even to have a chance of making it out of the forest I'd need the home-made tinder box to start my fires in the biting winds. I'd need the lighter, tucked back in Leon's bundle with everything else he'd stripped from the guard. I'd need—

Already I'd been away too long. Wanting more time to think, I started to retrace my steps. But it was only as I staggered out from under the overhanging branches towards the fire that the idea came.

'Out there,' I told them, pointing back through freshly spinning snowflakes. 'Out there is a dead bear.'

They both looked up. 'Dead bear?'

I nodded.

The two of them stared. 'Not rotted through the summer?' asked Leon, clearly finding it almost impossible to believe our luck. 'What, fit to eat?'

I shrugged, as if a youth spent in a prison camp had left me as short of wits as of spare flesh.

Already they were on their feet. After so long, a huge charred bear steak would be a feast indeed.

'How far?'

Again I shrugged like an idiot. Shaking their heads, they set off between the trees, following my foot-prints. I made great play of starting to come after, but neither took the trouble to look back. Even before they were out of sight between the trees, I'd snatched up the bundle in which Leon kept everything we had.

I looked around, taking my bearings. There was the way I'd pointed. Here was the track we should be following. And that left half a world of forest in which to hide myself.

But there was only one real choice – to stay on the track and keep ahead of my two desperate companions. They'd work that out soon enough. But to confuse them long enough for me to get round the first bend or two, I crossed the fire and hurled myself between the trees like a clumsy beast, showering off snow and snapping overhanging branches to leave them hanging raw.

A short way in I stopped and, using a spread branch, brushed at the footprints I made in the snow as I retraced my steps back to the camp fire.

The huge white swirling flakes would cover the last of both sets of tracks within moments. And during those moments I set off with Leon's bundle, silently and hastily along the track, still dragging the branch behind me to do the best job I could of brushing out my footprints.

CHAPTER EIGHTEEN

I've searched and searched, but can't find words to explain how strange it felt to pull apart that bundle, find the food those two had hidden, and feel no bitterness. How could I blame them? Shared even sparsely between them, the saved scraps wouldn't have lasted the length of the journey. So soon enough they would have needed their walking, talking larder – their amiable pillar of fresh meat, even content to carry himself along on his own legs till he was needed!

I couldn't blame them – not even for one shocked and angry moment. I had grown up. I'd lost all innocence. I'd come to learn that, in this world the Leader had created, two things had been so firmly set at one another's throats that no one could manage both. You could do right by others, or you could act cunningly enough to stay alive. Just look at me! I'd stolen the bundle. I had the gun, the tinder box to light my fires, the money from the guard's pocket and all that was left of the food. All that I had to do now was stay away from Leon and Oskar until they weakened and froze. Oh, they might forge ahead. They might go back. Or they might sit and despair. Oskar the Bear might even slide his beefy fingers around his old friend's neck. Cunning Leon might somehow trick his companion into falling so deep into a snowdrift that there would be no escape before he suffocated.

It made no difference. Meat or no meat, without a fire to keep their bodies from freezing, both would die.

And I felt nothing. No guilt. No pity. No triumph. Worst of all, no living interest in their fate, except insofar as it might touch on mine. All that I did was walk. I walked all night, not daring to stop and light a fire for fear of giving Leon and Oskar hope, from the faint smell of burning on the wind, that I wasn't far ahead. I walked all the next day, starting at every rustle in the forest, each slip of snow from a branch. Forcing my feet to be obedient, I tried to douse my terrors, and think of nothing but the crunch of snow and the moan of the wind in the trees.

I walked for seventeen days – seventeen days! – breaking the journey only to root through the last of the food in the bundle and light the fires that kept my own bones from freezing while I snatched the shortest of rests.

But mostly I simply put one foot in front of the other and told myself that there was nothing to be done except endure. This road was colder, fouller, even more dangerous than those before. But my whole life had gone down the wrong track. Nothing about it had ever been any choice of mine.

And that was nothing special. We were all slaves, walking a road of bones. Like everyone else in our benighted country, I was a cog in the machine. So why not simply plod and plod and plod between the trees, out between billowing mounds of fallen snow, then back between trees? If none of my short life had ever truly been my own, why not just plod, plod, plod?

And so I walked. Through everything: through frosty murk, winds strong enough to lean on, nights so black I might have feared my eyes had fallen out. I walked across crunching river beds, past dazzling snowdrifts and under skies ablaze with stars. I walked through air so translucent it seemed as if the world must have been born that very morning, and, within hours, through squalls of ice that beat so viciously they soaked through Gregory's long quilted jacket as easily as if it were made of tissue.

I'd light a fire, thinking of Leon and the Bear. In death, had they huddled close, their bodies crusted with ice? I'd warm my arms enough to bring back a little feeling, then peel off the jacket and stretch it over a frame of branches above the fire. I'd wear the guard's thick overcoat till that in turn was soaked through. On and on.

Days passed. The moon turned. And I kept walking. I kept the gun at hand, so desperate with hunger that I'd have risked wasting every last bullet if I'd seen one thing moving in all that ocean of white.

And then, one morning, I stumbled over a dead ptarmigan. Had the poor creature fallen, frozen, from the sky? So starved I couldn't wait, I feasted, half on charred skin, half on icy meat. Still, the food raised my spirits enough for it to seem that, after that day, the ice crystals swept less cruelly into my face. At times they turned to little more than snowy dust as the track twisted downwards – down, down, down – through pines, along the river creaking in protest beneath its thinning crust, down to a bridge.

From there, it widened. At last the fear was gone that I might mistake the way, and end up following some cart track into a dead-end forest clearing. Still the road wound down and down. I walked all night. By morning, when the blue-black of an almost starless night gave way to thin grey light, mists curled around me. On and on I went, until ahead of me I saw a thickening band of weak and yellow light.

It was the sun. Less than an hour later, the snow-fields on either side shone brightest silver.

Was that a bird? Was it *singing*?

I stopped. That's when I saw it in a cleft in the bank beside the road. A flower! A yellow flower!

Above it, snow lay in the cracks of rock like streaks of silver bullion. I raised my head. On the stiff breeze it flooded over me – the tang of the blessed spring melt! What lay ahead of me now in all that shining distance was nothing more than snow so lightly frozen it would crackle when I walked on it, a pale clear sun, and rivers bubbling through their winter crust.

I'd made it.

The air was filled with a crystalline freshness. Now there'd be fish to catch and game to ensnare. Soon I'd be walking over last year's pine needles instead of snow. And, sooner or later, walking across the gently stirring land that lay in front of me, I would find shelter.

It was a woodsman's hut. From the look of it it had been empty all winter, but under a pile of rags there lay a sliver of soap. Soap! I'd not seen soap in as long as I could remember.

Against the wall rested a shard of mirror so grimed with age I didn't realize that was what it was until I lifted it. I rubbed it clean and stood back to look.

The shock of it! I don't believe I would have recognized myself had I not grown to look so much like my own father. How I had aged and changed. Even my shorn hair was growing back nearer to grey than brown.

And that's where I stayed, coaxing the squirrels out of trees into the traps I found, roasting wood-cock and fish. To rid my body of lice, I scrubbed myself raw each morning, and stood beside the river to let the cold breeze dry my body while I watched the chunks of breaking ice go rushing past.

And I took stock. I had a gun. A hoard of bullets. The uniform of a guard. And hair grown long enough to pass. So there began a week of industry. I trimmed my hair more evenly with the sharp edge of a stone. I threw away the worst of my rotten footcloths, and washed the others, then tore them into such thin strips that I could weave them into something that might pass for proper boot linings. I cleaned the gun by rubbing grit from the river up and down its sides till it was gleaming. I flattened out the guard's cap and brushed the overcoat till it looked halfway to smart.

But then my courage failed me. There would be times when I'd be passing men in uniform – real guards, not easy to fool. Surely it would be wiser to travel in the quilted jacket I'd tossed in the corner. Lice eggs lay hidden in every seam and it would take more than one underwater beating to drive out so much dirt. But still I carried it down to the river's edge, studying the stitching doubtfully. Would it be strong enough to hold? This jacket of Gregory's had seen me through the fiendishly bitter weeks of middle winter and, if I were caught, the guard's coat would be ripped off my back in an instant. Should I be sent to any of a thousand camps, I'd need its warmth simply to stay alive.

I spread the jacket and ran my fingers over its dirt-caked pattern just the way I'd seen Gregory doing so often, sitting on his bunk.

A stiffness caught my attention. Was that an inner lining? But when I moved my hand across to the next quilted square, the sense of one more layer underneath was suddenly gone.

So. Not a lining.

I lifted the other sleeve and ran my fingers over that instead. And there was nothing to match.

Here was a mystery. We all had hiding places and our little secrets. What was it Gregory had wanted to keep so badly he'd sewn it into his jacket? And all those times I'd watched him run his fingers over his sleeve as if idly tracing the pattern, had he been checking something? Making sure it was still there?

Lowering my head, I pinched the jacket and bit through a stitch. I pulled out just enough thread to work a finger inside.

There were two folded sheets of paper.

I tugged at more stitches till I could pull them out. I flattened them on my knee.

Identification papers! Gregory's name and place of birth. His former occupation. Cabinet maker. How had he managed to keep them? Our papers were taken from us at the moment of arrest to make escape more difficult. Keeping them hidden in the way he had done must have earned Gregory more than one savage beating.

Why had he *bothered*? I brought to mind the gentle, hopeless man who'd coughed himself to death below my bunk, and thought I knew the reason. With Gregory, the sheer *stupidity* of his arrest was never out of his mind. The thought that his life had been destroyed for ever because of one stroke of the pen had seemed to him so monstrous, so far beyond belief, he'd felt obliged to keep the proof of it. Hadn't I heard him saying it a thousand times? 'How could I lose my wife and child, my job and home, and end up in this stinking hut? How could my life have boiled down to *this*?' Knowing the reason was hidden in that little square of quilt must be what had kept him sane: 'I'm not imagining this horror. Here under my fingers lies the cause. One scribbled number.'

I scoured it for the carelessly written date of birth that had derailed a good man's life and led to his early death. What had he told me he'd said to the official he'd begged to change it? 'Do I *look* eight years old?'

How long ago was that? How many years had Gregory rotted in the camps?

I peered at the year of birth as it seemed written, and tried to work it out. But to a boy whose only practice in numbers since he left school had been 'one load, and then one more, and then one more', the counting wasn't easy. It took a while to reach the answer.

And yet, how worth the effort!

Eighteen years old!

This was a gift indeed to a boy who might pass for anything from fourteen to twenty! Papers that suited!

Papers that might be handed over almost with confidence for inspection.

I put them safely under a stone and washed the jacket in the icy rolling water, remembering all the while how often Gregory had lain on his bunk and muttered bitterly, 'One careless little mistake! Enough to ruin a life!'

An error like this could prove to be a club with two ends.

Enough to ruin his life. But, if I stayed lucky, perhaps enough to salvage mine.

CHAPTER NINETEEN

Now there was nothing to be done but show more courage. I set off walking again, guessing that, since I'd not seen a living soul since leaving the forest, I must be days from a settlement. From time to time I'd see what looked like wisps of smoke in the distance, or some black smudge on a hill that might have been a man or a woman busy with sheep. But mostly there was nothing except hills thawing to a green almost unbearably bright to eyes so unused to colours, the bouncing spring breeze and, now the last of the powdery snow in the cart tracks had vanished, mud squelching underfoot.

Turning a corner, I saw a far-off figure and felt a wave of terror. Who was this stranger coming my way? A guard? A soldier? Perhaps even some other escaped prisoner ready to rob me of my bundle?

I didn't dare leave the path. To change direction or step aside would look suspicious. I didn't dare slow my pace. I simply let the figure draw so close that I could see the streaks of silver through his beard. My heart was thumping so loudly I was sure he could hear it.

Just as he passed, he raised a thumb to the sun and said in a voice so frail it might have been a sheet of paper rustling: 'Not so uncertain today.'

I nodded as eagerly as a doll with a broken head-spring. 'No, indeed!' I heard myself saying as I strode past him.

Safely past him!

Into my mind sprang one of my teacher's scoldings: 'Only a simpleton offers his fellow man no more than talk of the weather.' What did my teacher know? I felt as proud as if I'd passed the hardest examination! Indeed, I was still preening myself on my wits and repeating the clever exchange over and over – 'Not so uncertain today.' 'No, indeed!' – long after the two of us had become no more to one another than specks in the distance.

Puffed with the triumph of having passed so easily as just another stranger on the road, my boldness grew. Where better to practise the hardest deception than in this desolate place?

I pulled the uniform we'd stripped from the guard out of my bundle. 'I'll walk past just one person,' I told myself. 'Whoever it is, they'll not dare speak, and I won't even nod. I'll just stride past as if they're no more to me than the mud on my boots.'

With hands that shook, I put on the trousers and jacket. Even before I threw the overcoat across my shoulders, the sweat was pouring down. But as I pulled on the cap with that dread silver badge, my courage flooded back. So they were right, those old men in the camp! How many times had I heard them grumbling it as they struggled with warped saws and poorly mended hatchets? 'Just give a man the tool and he can do the job.'

Put on that cap, and confidence and vigour surge through your body like an electric charge. Behind that little silver serpent coiled to strike lies all the power of a hundred thousand vicious beatings. I swear I rose in stature. My stride was steadier on the road. After the years of trying to be invisible, I was astonished to find myself marching along almost with pride.

Then turning a bend to meet my very first challenge. It was a haggard woman carrying some bundle of her own. She kept her eyes down as she scurried past. I stopped to watch her hurry on, and even if she realized the steady sound of my footfalls had come to a sudden halt, she didn't dare turn.

'Too easy,' I told myself. 'One more – just to be sure,' and kept on walking down one long slope and up another, to the brow of the next hill.

Almost at once I heard the rumble of engines. A short way on, the track ran into a wide stony road. Keeping in the shadow of trees, I followed the road at my side as, trundling past, came lorry after lorry, closed and barred.

Still staying out of sight, I walked down yet another slope, and then another, till without warning I found myself stepping out under the struts of a watchtower.

Above me, a sentinel with a rifle was peering down.

I froze. Thinking myself back in my prisoner's rags, I waited for the rifle's sharp report and the last sting of flesh.

He took the briefest look, then, seeing me standing there in hopeless indecision, swung his rifle to the side.

It was an idle flick. What? Was he using it, not as a weapon but as a pointer? I glanced the way he'd shown and, sure enough, there was a sentry hut.

I could have run, but I'd have risked a bullet in my back. So, trapped, I walked towards the open doorway. From inside came the reek of fatty stew. A horribly scarred man with a mouth like a dark hole glanced up from his game of solitaire.

'Where to?' he asked me, reaching for the pad that lay beside his spread cards.

Where *to*? This was a harder test than talk of weather! And what a fool I'd been. Why wasn't I better prepared? Even as a guard, I needed a story to account for myself. I'd carried the uniform in my bundle for days – cursed its weight, taken the trouble to brush it clean and shine the buttons with a gritty rag. And then I'd wasted all that time admiring the flight of eagles and even flowers – flowers! – but not put a single moment aside to work out my story.

Or even consider the truth. Because, if I am honest, this was the moment I first realized that the thought of home was no longer in my mind. Too much had happened. I had been away too long. I'd seen too many horrors. Hope, longing, yearning – all of the thoughts and feelings that keep a man's heart alive were lost to me now. They'd brought me too much pain. I'd pushed them down so far it was impossible even to think of walking through the door into my mother's arms. Indeed, it no longer seemed possible that the old building in which I'd spent my childhood was even standing. My parents were surely long lost in all the country's bitter upheavals. And no doubt my grandmother lay, a heap of old bones, in an unmarked grave.

The only road was back. But as to where I might be headed, that was a mystery.

Still the guard was waiting. Laying down another card, he reached for the pen and looked up to ask with gathering impatience, 'Are you *deaf*? I asked, where to?'

And yet the future was a blank. The past was still too raw. All I could think of was the place I'd left. I stood and pawed the dirt like an anguished beast, unable to think of one single name except that of my own camp.

But then it came to me – a memory of Oskar drawing his map in the snow to show me where the train from the mines would meet the main line.

'To Treltsky.'

'A nice surprise!' he said scornfully, lifting the pad's mottled cover to reveal a hundred of those bright green slips I'd seen and envied so many times.

Rail travel permits.

He flicked to a few on which he'd already filled in some of the details. Even from where I stood, I could read the word 'Treltsky' on the one he tore from the pad. As he flattened it in front of him, the truth finally sank into my brain. I'd walked so far I'd met the railway line. The lorries rattling past must come from nearby mines. Some way beyond this hut must lie the track. And since the rail trucks only rolled this far to drop off prisoners or to pick up ore, the only ones to travel back on them were guards on leave, or off to some new posting.

Already his eyes were back on his cards. I'd watched enough solitaire to know his game had almost come out perfectly. Was that what saved me from any further questions – that and the fact that I'd chosen a destination so commonplace that this railway permit officer had already filled in the forms?

I reached for the voucher.

'Not so fast!' he snarled. 'I know your unit's little tricks – take it from me and sell it on to someone else! You sign it here – in my presence.'

He pushed the pen towards me. I stared at my right hand as if it were some small beast I couldn't trust. *Could* I still write? How many years had it been since I'd grasped anything other than the handles of woodsaws and axes.

It took a while before I could force my fingers closed around the pen. The sweat of fear seeped out of every pore. Press on, I ordered myself. For all you know, he'll think you're some overgrown peasant who learned his letters badly. He'll think it's foolishness, not fear, that's oozing out of you like fat from a roasting pig.

'Take your time!' he said sourly, laying one card on the next. But clearly my presence was distracting him because, with an oath, he whipped the top one off again and glared at me.

'Must you hang around all day?'

Stay calm, I told myself. He can't see into your head. He doesn't know your brain has shrivelled to nothing in a camp. He thinks you're stupid, so just struggle through.

Down they went, one by one, in letters so clumsy you'd think they'd been drawn by a child in his nursery.

Gregory Leonid Timorsch.

'Your papers?' he barked, shaking his head in wonder that he'd even had to demand them. 'And your Permission of Leave or Transfer.'

Papers, I had. But as for any Permissions, I was stumped. To give myself time to think, I started to root in my bundle. Should I turn and run? Or pull out the gun?

But he'd turned one more card, and his impatience got the better of him. 'Never mind!' he snapped, and pressed his official stamp down twice – once on my destination, and once on my pitiful handiwork.

He pushed the voucher towards me. Before my

clumsy fingers had even managed to scrape it off the desk, he was back to his game.

So there I stood. With papers. A uniform. A little money in my pocket. And a travel permit to Treltsky!

Now, for the very first time, I truly felt I might be headed for freedom. I hurried away, feeling my heart swell with a happiness so sharp it hurt. The flood of exhilaration could have lifted me from my feet, it was so strong. It was like growing wings.

The road turned. Stifling the impulse to move as usual into the shadow of trees, I forced myself to walk as boldly as any other man down one long open stretch of road and then round a bend.

There, in a valley, lay a huge workyard. Its slanted watchtowers were slung together with fences of barbed wire. Lorries rolled past the sentry post one by one. The place was a morass of carts and cranes and pallets, with scores of workers scurrying like ants.

And there, behind the fence, with jets of steam occasionally hissing, lay the great steam train that would carry me on the first step of my long journey home.

Can I describe it – that extraordinary feeling of watching the mountains behind me turn into hills, the forests become fields, the towering pines change back to aspen and birch? The train rolled over great rivers, some still carrying huge chunks of snow and ice down from the north towards the warming plains. That whole great sleeping land began to wake and breathe. It felt like a return to life.

I kept myself to myself, pretending to sleep when others came near. I left my place only to buy food from one of the starveling old biddies who seemed to appear out of nowhere whenever the train juddered to a halt. Strange feelings ran through me constantly. How odd it was not to feel perpetual hunger. How difficult to choose between this lump of bread and that (and how hard not to slide my arms round my choice to protect it when anyone came near).

I watched the land roll past – huge, endless – and thought back to the anthem I'd forced my parents and grandmother to sing all that long time ago, *Fairest of Lands*, about our nation's boundaries. I understood it now. Always before, my patriotism had been stiffened by terror. (Just one word out of place and I'd have earned a beating.) But this was something new – an admiration for a land so vast, so strong, that it could suffer almost anything. A land I now understood had been made even more noble by its evil sufferings. A land whose glories shone all the brighter for the bloody sacrifices from which they sprang.

This was a *different* sort of love of country, born in my own mind, forged by my own experience.

Heartfelt.

One evening, shortly after darkness fell, I heard the warning call. 'Treltsky! Treltsky Junction! All change!'

The train juddered to a halt. I gathered up my bundle and pushed the truck doors apart to gaze at this, the first real settlement on the way.

What had I been expecting? A golden city? Rivers of milk and honey running through? Chickens that fluttered to lay their eggs in my path? Sour cream in buckets?

It was a drab little town with only the sparsest lights dotted here and there on its plain grid. One pair of headlights juddered down a blacked-out street. A few dogs whined. Had this small place always been starved of kerosene, or had things worsened since I'd been away? No doubt Our Glorious Leader would still be knocking back his foreign wines, and stuffing his belly with rich imported foods. But clearly his blight lay just as heavily as ever on all the rest. I jumped down from the train, shaking my head in wonder. What sort of double book-keeping was this that made one man a king, and rated the lives of others so lightly that all their miseries could count for nothing?

I plodded up one street and down the next. All around loomed huge grey buildings, nine or ten storeys high, and yet the roads were no better than country cart tracks, scarred with the deepest potholes and running with mud.

Around the corner swept a brace of headlights – the first I'd seen since I stepped off the train.

Of course! A Black Maria. I flattened myself back in the shadow of a doorway, and out they poured, those men dressed just like myself.

I heard their grating voices. 'Up on the seventh floor. This side.'

'Is Popov round the back?'

'Oh, yes. He'll crush her into crowbait if she tries getting out that way.'

'Right, then!' I heard a laugh. 'On with the ferret chase!'

The clatter of their steel-tipped boots rang through the door and up the staircase. I shrank back further. But for the guard they'd left by the Black Maria, I would have run, prepared to trade the risk of being seen against the horror of watching some poor soul dragged out to suffer as I had. What had this woman and I done to find ourselves swept with such ease into the rubbish bin of history? Was it no more than bad luck that we'd been born in the hollow of such a poisonous wave? Was everyone living now supposed to comfort themselves that those born after might have better fortune, and live out their own days on some happy new crest?

The shouts grew louder. I heard the sound of wood splintering.

Way, way above, a casement window opened. A woman scrambled onto the narrow sill and stood, spreadeagled against the torchlights swirling behind her, shouting to rouse the dead.

'Wake up, all you good people! Take courage and support us! Join the fight! Freedom and justice!'

The guard on the street bellowed upwards. 'Grab her! Don't let her jump!'

But just before that sickening thud so very close in front of me, I heard the hunted woman's last brave cry.

'Yellow and Black!'

Chapter Twenty

I'll tell you this. Sow seeds of anger and bitterness deeply enough and what will bloom is utter fearlessness. I strode back to the station, stopping each person who passed.

'A pen? Have you a pen?'

One glance at my cap, and they'd have sold their souls for one to offer me. I had no time to make a play of kicking them for being empty-handed. I let them pass, still grovelling, and before they'd even scuttled down the next side street, astonished at their luck, I would be tackling another of those whose work shifts started long before dawn.

At last I had a pen in hand. Backing into a doorway, I took out the travel permit and stared.

Treltsky.

Preltsky?

Simple enough. A careful flick of the pen. And with a hundred thousand places in this vast country, who would be confident enough to pick an argument?

Within a shorter time than I could have imagined, I was back on a train, still travelling west. I had a red plush seat in a compartment for six, with lamps like glass dewdrops and a heater that would have doubled as a furnace in my old camp. The ticket inspector knew better than to ask to see my travel permit more than once, and all my fellow travellers stared anywhere except at the silver serpent on my cap, or into my eyes. I felt the authority of the uniform I wore in every furtive glance that shot my way. The insidious strength of it renewed my force of mind – though I was not so much of a fool as to forget it was a borrowed power, and one small trick of fate could once again turn my world upside down. I hadn't failed to notice that, linked on behind like poor rough cousins happily ignored, were trucks just like the ones I had been herded onto before, to travel east, now rolling back for more fodder for the camps, more men to work their fingers to the bone and bodies into the grave.

I could be one of those again.

But not the same man. I'd changed too much inside.

I spent my hours staring out through the window. Now there was more to look at: villages and towns – real towns, with schools and prisons, bands and parades, and busy factories. The things I saw as we rolled past! Once, on a sun-drenched platform, I watched a boy teasing a kitten with a ragged end of string and was astonished that the young still passed their time with empty-headed amusements. I saw a woman and her friend exchange a confidence, throw up their aprons and rock. That must be grief, I told myself. It can't be merriment. How could it be that, as one brave woman hurls herself from a window with a dying rallying cry, others can still be laughing at things so easily told? No, it's not possible. No, not with all these nightmares being lived along the track.

I watched it all – old men in tears, and women doubled under the loads they carried, dragging their wailing children. Try as I might, I felt no pity. I wanted to shake them from their ignorant dreams. 'You think your life's a misery?' I wanted to bellow through the compartment window. 'Think again! When you want water, you drink. You empty your bowels at will, not when you're ordered to do so. If you have lice, you've no one to blame but your own lazy self!'

By now, of course, they would be out of sight. But I'd still be staring back at where they'd vanished, thinking my murderous thoughts. 'Stupid, self-pitying peasants! When your feet bleed, at least you can sit by the wayside without fear of a bullet in your brain. And if you're lucky enough to have a lump of bread in the evening, at least you can hope there'll be more where that came from. You don't have to slave through the whole of the next day in icy blizzards, up to your knees in freezing slime, knowing for certain it will be hours and hours before you've half a chance of seeing even another crumb.'

And then I'd see a sight to soften me. The first mimosas. A glorious patch of willow herb. I'd gaze out into the blinding splendour of some bright morning and wonder what could ever have gone so wrong, that a country so rich in gifts could end up so dirt poor. As for the next Great State Plan! The next Stride Forward, the next Committed March! What sort of confidence could any leader have in any better future if he could send so many to rot for so long? I thought of the years marked down on our sentence sheets. Fifteen years! Twenty-five! Life! Anyone who truly believed that better times were on their way would be ashamed to write such numbers.

Get off the train, I tried to order myself. Cross the track. Go back the other way, to where you saw that clump of meadowsweet. Marry some pretty girl and tell yourself it's not your job to live out anything more than your own life.

But even a fool would snap himself out of such fairytale dreamings. There was nowhere to hide. And when had any of us been allowed to choose for ourselves where to live, or even what to do? The Glorious Leader had managed to turn this whole great country of ours into one giant *trap*.

And even as the word rang through my brain, the train began to judder. The wheels screeched to a halt.

I watched my five companions glance uneasily towards the window. The track was swarming with men in uniforms just like my own.

'Security check! Inspection! Out with your papers!'

Already those around me were rooting in their bags and pockets. The shouts grew closer. Yawning and stretching as if I'd had to face the fact that it was time to join my fellow guards and help with the inspection, I rose to my feet.

I slid the compartment door open and looked out. More guards with rifles stood along the track on the other side.

Brazen it out, I tried to tell myself.

But every instinct warned me. Not here. Not now. Instead, abandoning my bundle, I slid the door closed behind me and tried to walk along the narrow corridor past the other compartments with so much easy confidence that anyone who saw me would think I was one of the guards doing the check.

I worked my way to the back of the train and slid the bolt of the door that barred the way to the old viewing platform. Climbing the rail, I dropped down onto the large iron link that joined the prisoners' trucks to the passenger compartments.

I peered out on both sides. There was no chance of getting away unseen. So, choosing one side, I stepped out as casually as if I'd just ducked under the link from the other.

Cocking a thumb behind me, I said to the nearest guard, 'We've more men than we need on that side.'

He scowled. 'We'll never have more men than we need with this lot. They get stronger every day. Three trains derailed already this year. And then that bridge.' He shook his head. 'Yellow and Black! They have the cunning of weasels. They ought to change their colours. They should be grey and brown! That's what they ought to call themselves. Weasels!'

'True,' I said easily, moving off along the train and peering under each truck in turn to make a show of being part of the inspection. He showed no interest. Neither did the guard standing beside the next truck.

Or the next.

And it was on the underside of the truck after that

that I saw, unmistakably, that tiny little dewdrop of yellow paint I'd seen before, so long ago.

I lifted my eyes. Sure enough, though all the letters had faded over the years I'd been away, there were the words that I remembered, WE HAIL OUR GLORIOUS REVOLUTION, the last few letters painted by a different hand.

I couldn't help it. I had to look inside. With no ramp to climb, it was a bit of a scramble. No one stepped forward to help. The guards along the track watched with indifference as I forced the side door open.

The stink of sweat and herrings hit me like a brick. For pity's sake! Here, joined by no more than one strong link of metal, was my own past. My stomach clenched so tight, I nearly emptied everything I'd eaten that morning onto the floor. I heard the groans again. I saw the dead. I remembered the shouting. 'Water! Give us water!' I seemed to live the whole appalling journey in a moment before my wits came back.

I prowled around. Here's where I used to lie. There were the wooden slats that blocked the windows. I knew the tracery of their patterns better than I knew my own fingertips. How I must have grown! Back then, I'd had to stretch to peer between the two of them. Now I was forced to stoop.

I laid my fingers where they used to rest to save my eyes from splinters. The memories flooded back. The old man dying from a broken heart after his letter was spoiled. The long discussions deep into the night. The bursts of laughter. The times we tried to derail the train by hurling ourselves at its sides.

Liv Ullavitch's map. Yes! There it still was – those long thin lines gouged out along the side. Did the guards fail to see it for what it was when prisoners spilled out of the truck? Or had the transports followed one another with such grim haste that no one took the time to walk around? One simple swill of water, and back in service!

Outside, the tramp of boots was growing louder all the time. I heard raised voices, then an angry shout. 'What are you doing, standing around so idly?'

Clearly the guard tried to defend himself. 'Everything's checked.'

'Then check again, even more thoroughly! Check even one another's papers. A bundle's been found on the train, left by a man in uniform. Let no one you don't know pass!'

Fresh searchers were very close now. I hadn't spent so many weeks inside this truck without learning how to tell which doors were being slid open along the train.

Trapped!

Had I allowed the memories of past times to put an end to my future? I spun round. Nowhere to hide! Just wire cages in an empty truck. If I were caught, I might be dragged out but I'd soon be back, crammed in with a hundred other unlucky creatures.

The whole long nightmare would begin again.

In terror, I reached out to steady myself. I clung to the nearest wire. And suddenly another memory came back. I saw Liv forcing his way over the sleeping bodies to the side of the truck. 'Give me some room. I want to look out.'

What had his companions grumbled back at him? 'Keeping us waiting for some place that never comes?'

And he'd snapped back, 'Scoff at your own stupidity! You would have burrowed through your hole only to freeze to death!'

This time there was no straw over the floor. I knelt and peered where I remembered the two men always sitting.

By all the stars! The skill! The quality of workmanship. The care those two men had taken to feather the planks beneath them so carefully no one would ever know. Why had they even bothered to strew straw over their handiwork? Dozens of poor souls must have sat on this very spot and noticed nothing! What a crying waste!

I tore my fingers scraping at the years of dirt. I found the knothole cunningly designed to let in one small finger.

I raised the strangely shaped trapdoor and slid down onto the axle of the truck. Then, reaching up, I dragged the little raft of planks back over and twisted it round till, like a piece of jigsaw, the trapdoor fell back in place.

Almost at once I heard the scuffle of boots above my head.

'No one in here!'

May is the best month. May is the month I strolled through woods, teased the squirrels and stole from my countrymen. Whenever I needed something, I brushed down the uniform, put on the cap, and went to take it.

Everywhere I went, I asked about Yellow and Black. I'd stand so the sunlight flashed on the coiled serpent and spit out my questions. The frightened country folk tumbled over themselves in the rush to offer me answers – never, you understand, something they knew for themselves. Always something they'd heard.

I'd kick them around a bit. After all, hadn't I learned in the camp exactly how much beating a man could take, and how it might loosen a tongue? Perhaps I'd get to hear a little more. Perhaps I wouldn't. Still, three trains derailed in a single year in this one valley! As the days went by, I narrowed down the search. I knew that, sooner or later, the ones I planned to find would pass through again. I'd make myself known. Offer my services. How could they doubt my loyalty once I'd persuaded them of the truth of my past? How could they doubt that I would happily spend the rest of my life working to save my tortured country?

Above the valley was a tumbledown hut. I saw the woodsman off with threats of violence and arrest, and took his place. Day after day I watched till they finally came – the only ones truly to believe things could be different.

Yellow and Black.

When a man's youth has been kicked and starved out of him, it can't be put back. Compared to me, the rest were babes in arms. Good-natured innocents, as different from myself as I was from the old Yuri of long ago – that simple, cheerful boy who used to look at freshly fallen snow and think of happiness and freedom – snowballs and sleds – not freezing drudgery.

Like me, they knew how leaders can arise – that all it takes is a determination greater than that of those around you. Like me, they knew that those who won't lead must follow, or be ruled. But lacking the suffering that tempers a man of flesh and blood and feeling into pure steel, how could they pick up the burden?

Contact breeds trust. Trust brings responsibility. Responsibility leads to decision.

And orders are given.

But what are a few derailed trains when a whole country is broken? It was time to move on. The province first. Then, after that, we'd spread our wings wider and wider. So the day came to leave the valley and take our chances. I looked around the woods-man's hut one last time.

Was it pure chance that, just as I kicked a pile of rags aside, the sun shone in so strongly it showed the faintest hummock on the dirt-packed floor?

There! To sharp eyes, the tell-tale marks of digging. A careful stamping down.

It was a scrap of folded oilcloth, buried no deeper than the span of my hand. In it are coins, I thought. Perhaps a few precious stones. Or, at the very least, a useful knife. But when I unwrapped it, I found only a few coloured pages torn from a book.

I stared at them, mystified. And then I realized, from things my grandmother was hushed for saying, that they must be pictures of saints. Fat old saints! Nothing more useful! Yet buried so carefully!

Back in the camp there'd been a saying: 'A prisoner on the run is like a baby: whatever he sees, he wants.'

Not so, I told myself. They might be precious to some ignorant woodsman who spent his summers here. But they're quite useless to me. A memory came back of Igor in that roofless cottage in the woods, waking at night to read his greasy Bible. Were all these grizzled folk's minds as wrinkled and empty as their skins, that they should take such risks to stick to old ways of thinking?

For there could be no God – certainly none worth bowing your head before, or kneeling to worship. In a world stuffed with horrors, such a ghostly overlord must either care for no one, or have no powers. In either case, why would these rheumy-eyed ancients risk their lives to hide his keepsakes? So far as I could tell, life was no more than a stretch of misery between two empty secrets. What was the stubbornness that lay in all these old folk, that they would cling so tightly to their God?

And as I reached the door, the answer came. Perhaps, like Grandmother, they'd realized right from the start that paradise can't be built on earth – especially not with fear for bricks, and threats for mortar. Maybe if you'd been raised on all the mysteries of miracles and angels, these 'great truths' spouted by Our Glorious Leader had never seemed other than nonsense. Perhaps this 'Shining Future' dangled before us as a bribe had always appealed to them no more than some cheap bauble on a market stall.

What would they think of what I had to offer?

Easy enough to guess!

And those – like my parents – who'd reckon they'd seen it all before. What would they think?

The answer was plain. Small wonder any thoughts of going home had vanished into air. How could you put your mind to gaining power if you were haunted by a look in your mother's eyes, the sound of your father's sigh?

So should I go on? Would it be right or wrong to drag the country through another tide of bloodshed? People will always have failings. Reach for perfection and maybe the killing will never, ever stop.

Which was the right path to take?

It wasn't possible to judge. The old scales were

broken. The day the Leaders locked up the churches they'd ripped out God's own 'good' and 'bad' and left an emptiness their false beliefs rushed in to fill. Man made the choices now. The person with the greatest power decided for us all where 'guilt' and 'innocence' lay.

For Our Great Helmsman, it was with some test of his own called 'social danger'.

There would be time enough to learn what it would be with me.

But I had given orders. It was time to leave. The pictures of saints fluttered across the damp floor. Already their colours had begun to seep, and by the time the woodsman lifted them out of the mud they would be ruined.

Why not? Why shouldn't the old fossil share the common misery? Why should he wriggle out of what the rest of us suffered simply because, as a child, he had been taught to believe in some Maker who knew his name and loved him? God and his saints indeed! Unreal as shadows thrown across a wall to comfort a crying child. Why shouldn't this old woodsman, just like the rest of us, be forced to strip his notion of himself down to the realization that he was no more than a cog in some vast national machine? A creature no more valuable – and quite as easy to crush – as an ant.

For that's what the Leader had made of all of us! That's what we were! To change things for the better would take a sternness and determination equal to his.

And this time we would get it right. There'd be no loss of nerve, no half measures and no falling short. To reach the goal, we'd need the efforts and conviction of every single citizen: the young; the strong; even the old. Not even weak-minded back-pedallers like this old woodsman could be left to wallow in their hollow comforts. Things were now desperate. So everyone must join the struggle, and those who weren't with us – Yellow and Black – might as well be against us. Oh, all that long time ago I'd slid that other old believer's greasy Bible back into his mattress without a thought. But not any more! If life in the camp had taught me anything at all, then it was this: keep to the rules of the nursery, and things would stay for ever as grimly insupportable as they were now.

A simple, never-ending road of bones.

So they would have to be taught. New aims. New drills. New banners. Yellow and Black. Everything they thought they knew would have to be uprooted.

We'd take a leaf out of the Leader's book. He knew the score. He'd used them all: imaginary terrors, empty promises, bright slogans. We would waste no more time. We'd plaster posters on every wall and paint our enemies in such dark colours that no one could fail to despise them. To build our new country, with freedom and justice for all, we would make pitilessness our only right, and pity our only wrong.

For I was a man of conviction now. A true believer. And so all leniency must be pushed aside. No more indulgence. Just as a general in command must send some units off to certain death to save the battle, so anyone who wanted to rid our land of evil might have to sacrifice what he had thought till then was simple kindness. The end would justify the means, and if those too stupid to understand the aim in view had to be whipped into seeing that they'd been beaten for too long, then whipped they must be.

I glanced down at the pictures still bleeding colours into the dirt. Saints! Harebrained distractions! The spawn of nonsense. Nothing but stardust in the eyes to blind people to the real truth!

In my mind's eye, I saw the owner of the hut creep back and lift the latch. I watched him weep to find his precious pictures on the floor, sodden and spoiled. I could have wept myself.

Then, Nonsense! I told myself. How much of a lesson in resolve could I have learned if causing the colours on a picture to run unnerved me more than thoughts of all the blood still to be spilled?

I ground the pictures to pulp as I strode out. But still I found myself, all that long day, hearing the echo of my grandmother's scorn: 'Only a fool cheers when the new prince rises,' and caught myself walking faster, and ever faster, as if to get away from my new self.

ABOUT THE AUTHOR

ANNE FINE was born in Leicester. She went to Wallisdean County Primary School in Fareham, Hampshire, and then to Northampton High School for Girls. She read Politics and History at the University of Warwick and then worked as an information officer for Oxfam before teaching (very briefly!) in a Scottish prison. She started her first book during a blizzard that stopped her getting to Edinburgh City Library and has been writing ever since.

ANNE FINE is now a hugely popular and celebrated author. Among the many awards she has won are the *Carnegie Medal* (twice), the *Whitbread Children's Novel Award* (twice), the *Guardian Children's Literature Award* and a *Smarties Prize*. She has twice been voted Children's Writer of the Year at the British Book Awards and was the Children's Laureate for 2001-2003.

She has written over forty books for young people, including *Goggle-Eyes*, *Flour Babies*, *Bill's New Frock*, *The Tulip Touch* and *Madame Doubtfire*. She has also written a number of titles for adult readers, and has edited three poetry collections.

Anne Fine lives in County Durham and has two daughters and a large hairy dog called Harvey.

www.annefine.co.uk

anne Fine

the Book of the Banshee

It's war ...

Will has two sisters.
Muffy – a little angel who loves bedtime stories.
And Estelle.
A screaming, screeching banshee whose moods
explode through the household.
Mum and Dad have surrendered.
And Will feels as if he's living on the front line ...

A hilarious tale from multi-award-winning
author Anne Fine.

'Anne Fine has a subversively wicked gift for exploring
family tensions' *Independent*

A Corgi Book
978 0 552 55303 2

www.kidsatrandomhouse.co.uk

aNNe FiNe

On the Summerhouse Steps

A girl with Notions.
A lovelorn student.
And Ione, alone in the summerhouse, pondering the
Meaning of Life.

Add one eccentric professor for a sunny extravaganza
of chocolate fudge cake, strawberries – and a mad
moon-dance at midnight.

And that's just the beginning . . .

Sparky new editions of multi-award winning
author Anne Fine's first two novels, THE SUMMER-HOUSE LOON
and THE OTHER DARKER NED.

'Extraordinary and hilarious events' *Guardian*

'Deep understanding, wisdom and compassion . . . tosses
the reader between laughter and tears with expert dexterity'
Junior Bookshelf

A Corgi Book
978 0 552 55269 1

www.kidsatrandomhouse.co.uk

ANNE FINE

Round Behind the Ice House

Something is dying – a closeness . . .

Cass and Tom are twins, as alike as two peas in a pod.
Bound by the secrets they have shared in the old ice house.
For ever.
That's what Tom thinks.
It's not what Cass wants.
Not any more . . .

A gripping tale of passions and loyalties.

'A very real sense of menace' *Guardian*

'Striking' *Sunday Telegraph*

A Corgi Book
978 0 552 55268 4

anne Fine

Up On Cloud Nine

How stupid do you have to be to fall out of a
top-floor window?

Or was Stolly trying something else?
Up on cloud nine.
It's up to his best mate, Ian, to find out the truth . . .

HIGHLY COMMENDED FOR THE CARNEGIE MEDAL

'(A) brave and sometimes brilliant book' *Independent*

'A tour de force – moving, funny, pacey and profound' *Guardian*

'Subtle and entertaining . . . will make children of both
sexes accept unusualness and difference, both in
themselves and others' *Sunday Times*

A Corgi Book
978 0 552 55465 7

www.kidsatrandomhouse.co.uk